THE
TRAP

THE TRAP

STEVEN ARNTSON

HOUGHTON MIFFLIN HARCOURT
Boston New York

www.hmhco.com

The text was set in Weiss.

Library of Congress Cataloging-in-Publication Data
Arntson, Steven, 1973–
The trap / by Steven Arntson.
p. cm.
Summary: In 1963, when twins Henry and Helen and their best friends, Alan and Nicki, try to find Alan's missing brother, Carl, they stumble into the knowledge of their "subtle forms" that can separate from their physical bodies, and into a criminal's plot to make himself immortal — at any expense.
ISBN 978-0-547-82408-6
[1. Supernatural — Fiction. 2. Best friends — Fiction. 3. Friendship — Fiction. 4. Brothers and sisters — Fiction. 5. Twins — Fiction. 6. Family life — Iowa — Fiction. 7. Iowa — History — 20th century — Fiction.] I. Title.
PZ7.A7415Tr 2015
[Fic] — dc23
2014010211

Manufactured in the United States of America
DOC 10 9 8 7 6 5 4 3 2 1
4500522506

CHAPTER 1

THE LAST DAY of summer break before the start of my seventh grade year was the first time I ever got punched in the face.

It was August 1963 and a hot, humid summer afternoon outside of Farro, Iowa. I don't know if you've been to southeast Iowa, but in summertime going outside here can be like walking into a lung. I once saw a guy in a grocery store parking lot faint into his own shopping cart.

"Why are we spending the last day of vacation trying to help Carl?" I complained, wiping sweat from my brow as we four (me and my sister Helen with our best friends Alan and Nicki) pedaled along an easy slope. "He beat up Ernest last week." Ernest wasn't a personal friend of mine, but he was a good example of someone Carl Dunn had recently clobbered. Every kid around Farro was anxious about Carl, and not in the sense of worrying about his welfare. He was the worst bully in Johnson County, and he'd gotten twice as bad this summer, almost like he was taking lessons. I was terrified of him, and plenty nervous about scouting around for his secret hideout. But I was willing to, all the same, mainly because Carl was Alan's older brother, and Alan was my best friend.

Alan and Carl were mostly opposites. Carl was tall and Alan was short. Carl was dumb; Alan was smart. Carl was a bully who ruled the whole town of Farro with threats and violence. Alan was a nice kid, friends with almost everyone. The only things the two of them shared were their dark summer tans and high batting averages—the first because they were both part Nez Perce Indian, and the second because they both took after their dad when it came to baseball. Myself, I was terrible at baseball. Also I never tanned, only burned.

There was one other reason I was out here today— Helen's best friend Nicki pedaling beside me as we turned onto North Half, a dirt lane that edged the lip of Long-belly Gulch.

Nicki's bike was blue, with red tassels on her handle-bar grips. Her tires were the kind with white sidewalls, streaked with dirt from a busy summer. I studied her bike because I was too nervous to study her. She was right there, wearing sandals, muscly smooth brown legs, red shirt, shiny black hair, button nose, but I couldn't take more than a sidewise glance, because I would've crashed.

I had a crush on her. I'm not sure when it started, and at this point maybe it didn't matter. It took a lot of energy for me to act normal around her, so I focused on that.

When Nicki put on a burst of speed, I followed. We came neck and neck with Helen and left Alan trailing. Alan's bike was in sad shape. He'd inherited it from Carl years ago. There were broken spokes front and back, and the rear axle didn't have any lug nuts so sometimes the wheel fell off. It was less of a bike and more of a bike accident.

Helen and I rode brown ten-speeds, identical except mine was boy's style with the straight top bar and hers was girl's style with the angled top bar so she could ride while wearing a dress. (Not that she was wearing a dress. She never wore one during summer vacation.) Identical bikes are one of those things that happen when you're twins, even girl and boy twins. Two of everything. Twins are always plural, like pants or scissors. Nobody thinks of a single pant, or just one scissor.

Our bikes were a little small. We were supposed to get new ones this year for our birthday, but Mom and Dad couldn't afford them. Dad's job at the rail yard was giving him fewer hours, and we were having to "tighten our belts," Dad said. Keeping two old bikes was the equivalent of two notches on the family financial belt, I believe.

Helen's bike had a racing stripe and flames painted on, which she'd done when she got it, angry about it being girl's style. She said I should have gotten the girl's-style bike, and maybe she was right, since she liked to go off jumps and I didn't. Helen was also always quick to point out that she was twenty minutes older than me. In general, she was the boss of us. For instance, when this plan of seeking out Carl's hidden campsite was first presented by Alan, I'd said, "We should think about this first," which is what I usually say. Then Helen had grabbed my ear and dragged me outside—her usual reply.

North Half reeked of oil because around here they oil dirt roads in the summer to keep the dust down. I'm not sure which is worse, the stench of the oil or the dust, but I guess the people who spread the oil must hate the dust.

We juddered over the potholes and Alan's wheel fell off, but he caught himself and replaced it so quickly I don't think he ever came to a full stop. The juddering made me feel more nervous. I'd meant it when I'd said I wanted to think this through, and I would have felt a lot better if we'd taken a few moments at the kitchen table to brainstorm a quick pros and cons list. Writing things out always helps me. But for Helen it seemed like the opposite. Writing things down, for her, was like standing around after hearing the starting gun.

North Half was widely known by kids around here, an abandoned track along the gulch's edge. It went, ultimately, nowhere. I mean, it probably had a purpose once, but that once and that purpose were ages gone.

Eventually, the road became too rough to ride. We stashed our bikes in the brush and continued on foot.

"How far, Alan?" Helen asked.

"Past the gulch, I think. In the forest," said Alan.

I walked next to Nicki. Out of the corner of my eye I studied her sandals, which showcased her two perfect sets of toes.

"Whew!" I said, conversationally. In avoiding a direct gaze, I caught other glimpses—a knee shining with sweat, her upper arm, her black hair stark against her graceful brown neck. She seemed to glow when she sweated. When I sweated I felt like a baked potato.

"Hurry," said Nicki. "Helen's running!"

Helen was way ahead of us in her eagerness to get into trouble.

To our left, Longbelly Gulch opened up, and to our right, Longbelly Prairie, a wide bowl on the shaded north-facing slope. Although it was afternoon, a thin mist hovered over the grasses out there. I saw some cardinals and bluebirds, and heard a woodpecker whacking a trunk.

You might think Iowa is just a big corn farm full of tractors, but in southeast Iowa there are beautiful gulches and hillsides of prairie. Longbelly Gulch was so called because it looked like a big long belly pressed into the hillside. At the bottom ran Longbelly Creek.

Once we passed the field and entered the maple forest, we came to a berm at the edge of the road, covered in clumpy seeding grass that was beaten into a trail. I looked at Helen to see what she made of it, since she was our lead adventurer.

My sister is about my height, and I guess she and I look similar. People say so. We're blond and skinny and we tend to dress the same, especially during the summer. That said, I often feel like she's better than me. She doesn't look awkward in her body. Her ears don't stick out as far as mine (and she grows her hair over them anyway). I've always thought that for the twenty minutes after Helen rushed out to be born, I was sitting in the womb, debating whether or not to follow.

Helen led the way off-road into the forest. As we walked, an eerie sound came up. It was a little like a violin, a steady tone that went up and down in pitch, caused by two branches somewhere overhead scraping against each other. Right after we heard the sound, we found what we were looking for—the campsite. We ducked down and peeped through the trees.

There was a dirty mattress on the ground and two black scars of old campfires with white hubs of ash. Behind a tree I saw a corner of blue fabric, maybe a sleeping bag, shoved into a stump. Next to that, a cardboard box stained with water. I definitely did not want to meet Carl out here.

Helen stepped in like she owned the place, and the rest of us followed. The musical branches called down from overhead, as if to warn that whatever happened from here on out would be our own fault.

"What do you think he's doing out here, Alan?" said Helen.

"I don't know," said Alan. "But I think he's getting into something he shouldn't be."

"I hope we can help out," I said. Of course, helping Carl was a priority for me only because Alan was worried about him. But that was enough.

"The thing is, you guys," said Alan, "I, um, found his diary. And read some of it."

"Carl keeps a diary?" said Helen. That's what we all were thinking — Carl didn't seem like the diary type.

"More like notes to himself," said Alan. "In a yellow spiral notebook. He'd hidden it, but I almost think he wanted me to find it."

"What was in there?" I asked.

"He mentioned this place," said Alan, "and other stuff, too. Weird lists of numbers, like '1, 1, 2, 3, 5 . . . ' Then there was a label, 'Stakeout,' underlined, with stuff like 'Left home 1 p.m.' or 'Grocery store 3 p.m.' The last was 'Ambulance arrived 5 p.m.'"

"He was spying on someone?" I said.

"Yeah," said Alan. "And he was doing it *for* someone, I think. Because there was one line that said, 'Meet Abe 7 p.m., Old Road.'"

"Where's the notebook now?" Nicki asked.

"Carl found me reading it," said Alan. "He didn't get

very angry, but he took it, and I haven't been able to find it again."

Helen and Nicki walked to the old mattress, and Helen gave it a kick. Alan and I went to the dead campfires. "How long you think these have been burned out?" he asked.

"Not long," I said. I had no idea how to estimate the age of a campfire, but sometimes it just feels good to sound smart. I picked up a stick and poked the ashes. "Maybe two days," I said.

"Hey you guys," said Helen, beckoning to me and Alan. She'd just reached into the cardboard box next to the mattress, and now held a pile of damp-looking paperback books in one hand.

I stepped over and picked one off the top. The sweet smell of moldy pages wafted up. The cover showed a man in a space suit aiming a laser gun at a giant drooling centipede. The title, in capital letters that looked like lightning bolts, read *AIRMAN CRUSADER VERSUS THE CENTIPEDE KING*. The author was A. Møller—the "o" with the slash through it that happens with Norwegian names, which always makes me think of the empty set from math class.

"These are all the same series," said Helen, looking at

the spines. Nicki took the next one, whose title was *AIR-MAN CRUSADER VERSUS THE BAT CREATURES*, and she said, "You ever read these kinds of books, Henry?"

"Sure," I said. I liked pretty much any kind of adventure book. I read lots, and no sooner did I see these than I wanted them, especially because Mom had been limiting my trips to the bookstore for the past few months, as a belt-tightening measure. "Do you think they're Carl's?"

"Who knows," said Helen. "Let's take 'em." She shoved them at me to put into my rucksack, which I did. I always carry a rucksack. Helen never does. I guess I'm her rucksack.

She glanced a final time around the site and said, "All right, we've seen it. Let's go."

I was relieved. We left quickly and returned to the road, then to our bikes.

Where Carl was waiting for us.

CHAPTER 2

GETTING HIT IN THE FACE made me feel suddenly thoughtful. I sat down. This often happens with me. When I have a new experience, I need to take a minute to mull it over. Decide how I'm going to react.

First question: What happened?

Answer: Carl's big knuckles had come at me, his pimply face looming behind them. Then there'd been the stretchy sensation of the skin of Carl's knuckles shoving the skin of my nose and cheek. My nose and cheek backed up—right into my brain, and my brain retreated down my throat into my stomach. My stomach hadn't expected that, and became upset.

Second question: What should I do?

Answer: I should barf.

I leaned over and pitched my lunch into the dirt. As I took an extra moment to see if my brain was in there, I heard a voice yelling at me. "C'mon, Henry," it said. It was

Helen. A special urgency in her tone pulled me out of my own situation to take a new look around.

Things had changed since I got hit. I was pretty surprised. I'd assumed that everyone else had taken a break, like I had, to think it all over, but this wasn't the case.

Nicki was next to me on the ground. Her long black hair was in tangles, and tracks of tears smeared with dust blotted her cheeks. A few feet away, Alan was getting up from where he'd been knocked down. He was yelling, and at first his words made no sense to me. I'd have expected him to say something like, "Leave us alone, Carl," but what he actually yelled was, "Leave him alone, Helen!" This brought me to the final element of the scene.

Carl was a big kid, over six feet tall and with arms as thick as my legs. He looked like he'd been forged in a steel mill. At the moment, though, he was on one knee, gasping for air around Helen's chokehold. She was latched onto his back, her feet dangling. She was yelling at me because I was sitting so close I could easily have punched him right in the gut, which probably would have ended the fight.

But I'm not that guy. I just can't react quickly in stressful situations, and so I wasted the few seconds I had by staring stupidly as Carl gurgled and slung my sister around like a cape.

The one who finally acted was Alan, and he did not do what Helen was hoping for. Instead, he rushed to his horrible brother's defense, dragging Helen off of him and falling into the dirt with her.

Carl sprang to his full height, triumphant as a jack-in-the-box. He hadn't even noticed how close he'd come to losing, or that he would've been strangled if his brother hadn't rescued him. No, he was deciding that he'd just cleaned our clocks. He held up his long arms and bellowed, at the top of his lungs, "I'm gonna live forever!"

It was a weird thing to shout, but the victor can choose his victory cry. Then he turned and ran off along the old road, probably out toward his campsite. I think he had no idea that we were just coming from there.

We were wrecked. All of us, except Helen, were in tears. I felt ashamed because my only contribution to the fight had been to puke. Nicki hadn't fared much better, but she also hadn't been positioned right in front of Carl's exposed belly and missed the chance.

Alan was the first to speak, even as we were all still pushing hair out of our eyes and spitting grit. "You could have really hurt him," he growled at Helen.

"I was trying to save you!" said Helen, aghast.

Alan cursed under his breath and took a step away as if he were about to storm off.

"Alan," I said, grabbing his arm, "c'mon. We're all mad. We gotta calm down."

Alan shook my arm off but he didn't leave. "I hate him," he said finally, which was a little more in line with how the rest of us were feeling. He took a handkerchief from his back pocket and wrapped it around the bloody knuckles of his right hand.

"Um, anyone want an orange soda?" I said. "Cold orange soda at our house."

CHAPTER 3

I TALKED UP the orange soda as we rode back through the sweltering afternoon. I described the cool glass bottles in our fridge, rattling in the door, and the refreshing sensation of orange soda bubbling down a parched throat. Then I remembered that we were out of orange soda. Orange soda had been declared a casualty of belt-tightening.

Our home is an old farmhouse with a white picket fence out front. Not much to say, it's nothing special, especially when it's got no orange soda.

We parked our bikes out front and I led the way in through the kitchen screen door, calling to see if Mom or Dad was home. Neither answered.

"I wish my house was empty like this sometimes," said Alan. I wasn't sure if he was referring to his brother Carl or to his father. Could've been either.

I rushed to the back of the kitchen and threw open the refrigerator door, and saw, to my surprise, a ton of orange soda on the second rack. Dad must have bought it just to be nice. We each drank a whole bottle in a gulp. As our blood filled with fizz, we opened a second round and sat at the kitchen table.

"Henry, I think when Carl punched you it made your ears stick out more," said Helen.

"What? No," I said. I pushed at my ears, which I was always a little self-conscious about.

"You're gonna have a black eye tomorrow," said Alan.

"Henry, was that the first time you've ever been hit?" said Nicki.

"You threw up," Alan observed.

"Let's stop talking about me for a second," I said, and then added, *Burrrrp!*

"I'm sorry, you guys," said Alan. "I know Carl can be a jerk. But he's my brother." *Burp.*

"He has really been extra bad this summer" — *bellllch!* — said Helen.

"And he didn't show up for practice yesterday," said Alan.

Carl was a senior at Johnson High, and on the varsity baseball team. He was a great hitter, and a great first baseman — like Alan. They took after their dad, who'd been a pitcher in the majors, playing for the Twins until he hurt his back a few years ago. All to say, baseball is huge in their family. And even though it was just an off-season practice and didn't count for much, it was pretty surprising that Carl would miss it.

"Does your dad know?" Helen asked.

"Doubt it," said Alan, shaking his head. Alan's dad wasn't very interested in stuff. Like, not really interested in life at all beyond watching baseball on TV. His back bothered him, so he spent most of his time on the couch in their living room. But he did care about his kids. He'd be concerned if he knew Carl was skipping baseball.

"Who do you think this Abe guy is, Alan?" Nicki interjected. "And what are they doing out there in the woods?"

"Aside from reading science fiction books," said Helen, frustrated that we hadn't found any real clues.

"I wish I could find that notebook again," said Alan. "There was an address there, maybe the person Carl was spying on."

Just then, a noise came from the living room.

Helen and I knew the sounds of our house really well, and she was quick to respond. She leaped from her chair saying, "Gottago," and she was gone, the screen door slamming behind her only after she'd jumped on her bike outside. She was too fast for me. I was still halfway through recognizing the sound as Dad getting up from the living room couch. I hadn't even got to thinking about how this meant he'd be working a shift at the rail yard tonight with Mom. And that being the case, he'd want Helen and me to make dinner to put in the fridge for when they got back. Consequently, as usual, Helen had left me to do it myself.

Dad came through the kitchen door and saw me, Alan, and Nicki sitting around the table, all of us looking after Helen.

"Hello, Mr. Nilsson," said Nicki and Alan together.

My dad is a tall, thin guy with blond hair in a crewcut. He used to be in the army, and he told me once, as a joke I think, that the army has a way of cutting your hair so it never grows again. Ever since he got back from serving in Korea he's had this super-short hair. His ears stick out, too, kind of like mine. I got that from him.

A couple of expressions passed across Dad's face as he looked at us, one on the heels of the next. First, he was obviously about to tell me to cook dinner. He always did this in a stern way, because once I'd whined that I didn't want to, and now I thought he always expected me to complain. But this expression vanished in favor of a surprised look, as he saw my punched eye. He squinted like he did sometimes when the car wouldn't start—focusing in on an unwelcome problem.

"It wasn't my fault, Dad—" I began, which is a really bad way to start explaining something. Why is it that when you say it's not your fault, it sounds like it is?

"You were fighting," said Dad. There was no denying it. All three of us were pretty banged up. "You two go on home," Dad said to Nicki and Alan, gesturing at the door.

They stood, both glancing at me empathetically. "See you tomorrow," said Alan.

"See you later, Henry," said Nicki.

They left, the screen door letting in a puff of hot air from outside as it closed behind them, and Dad and I were alone.

This was potentially serious. Nothing made Dad angrier than fighting. He had absolutely forbidden Helen and me to fight, ever, no matter what. It had been his position since he got back from Korea. The first day he came home after his tour ended, he hugged us both right here in the kitchen and said, "Neither of you is ever to fight, and neither of you is to join the military. Do I make myself clear?" Those were the first words he said to us. Only later did he tell us that he'd missed us, and loved us.

I have no idea what happened to Dad during the war. He's never talked about it, but it all made a very bad impression on him. He didn't want anyone to ever fight about anything for the rest of all eternity.

Dad sat at the table with me, and he didn't say anything for a second.

"Thanks for getting soda," I said. Here's the thing about my dad—he gets angry easily, but not always. It's unpredictable, so it's worth it to see if you can do something to calm him down.

Dad nodded, and I could tell he was glad for the thank-you. "Did the paper come?" he asked.

Without a word I jumped from my seat and ran outside to check—and the paper was there, rolled in a rubber band and leaning against the bottom step. I picked it up and worked out the creases.

There were three articles on the front page. One headline read, "Washington March Organizers Expect Peaceful Demonstration." Another said, "Unions Gridlocked Over Rail Contract." The third one said, "Noted Philanthropist Died Saturday." Two of these were not going to be of interest to Dad. And the one about the union didn't sound promising.

Dad took the paper from me and mumbled under his

breath as he stood and headed to the living room — telling me to make dinner and put it in the fridge, because he had a late shift with Mom.

I breathed a sigh of relief. He hadn't gotten mad. But after I thought about it for a second, I realized there was still some peril here for me and Helen. Dad knew we'd been fighting, and he'd surely tell Mom, and probably get riled up again unless I could provide a decent explanation.

So, even though I didn't want to, I followed him into the living room. He was sitting on the couch across from the TV set, just starting to read the front page.

"Um, Dad?" I said. "About the fight. I have to tell you."

He didn't look up, but I knew his big scoop ears were hearing every word. "I didn't fight at all," I said. "I just got hit."

"That's still fighting," he replied, clearly not wishing to get further into it.

"No," I said. "It's . . . um . . . nonviolent noncooperation." I thought this was pretty clever, a term I'd picked up from the news recently about civil rights demonstrations in the South. "I swear, Dad, scout's honor." I raised my hand, though I'd never been a Scout.

"Who hit you?" said Dad, lowering the paper and thus signifying his willingness to transfer his disapproval to my attacker. I felt weird admitting it was Carl, since he's Alan's brother and I didn't want Alan to look bad. But there was nothing for it.

"Carl Dunn," I said.

Dad frowned, then shook the paper and raised it again. "Dis-missed," he said to me, like a drill sergeant. I turned and left the room, feeling sorry for Alan for having such a jerk brother, and still not exactly sure where things stood with my father.

Dad wasn't home for much longer than it took him to read the A section. Within thirty minutes he was passing back through the kitchen, dressed in his gray work outfit with the Burlington Northern logo on the pocket.

I was, at that moment, looking at a recipe book in the kitchen, having cleared away the empty pop bottles. "What did the article say about the strike?" I asked.

"Nothing," said Dad. (It was amazing how often our newspaper said nothing, and yet my parents never canceled their subscription.)

After Dad left, my thoughts stayed with him for a while. He used to work full-time for the Burlington

Northern Railroad as a fireman. You might think of a fireman as someone who puts out fires, but a fireman on a railroad is the opposite. He keeps a steam engine powered up on a steam locomotive. There weren't so many steam locomotives these days, though—they were mostly diesel. So the company wanted to get rid of firemen, but the union contracts said firemen had to be part of crews. The company had reduced Dad to part time, working nights whenever he could get them. Now Mom, employed by the company as a night clerk, was earning most of the money for us, which wasn't much. I knew it was stressful. They argued about money sometimes, and of course Helen and I had not gotten new bikes this year, and some other things.

As I thought, I cooked. I decided to make chili. I emptied two cans of tomatoes and two cans of red beans into the crock pot and then added onions, carrots, ground beef, and plenty of chili powder—I'd heard spicy food helps you cool down on a hot day.

Once the chili was simmering and the kitchen was full of good sneezy smells, I went into the living room. I lay on the couch, and my mind immediately returned to the fight. I remembered Helen yelling, and I remembered standing dumb while my opportunity passed. As I relived the humiliation, my ears felt hot and my eye throbbed.

And then I did something that often helps me to feel a little better. I got a pencil and a piece of paper and wrote it all out. Only, I didn't write it the way it happened. I wrote it the way I wished it had happened. In this version, Carl punched me but I wasn't fazed. I came back quick with a sock to the nose and he fell over, crying, butt in the air. I put a foot on his neck, turned to Nicki, and said, "Wanna go to the dance?" Nicki batted her eyes at me . . .

My pencil skidded and stopped. It was getting too unrealistic. I wished I was the kind of person who really could do stuff like that—take charge of the situation while it was happening, and not sit around wishing and dreaming hours later. If only, I thought to myself, I was more like my sister. I crumpled the paper, threw it at the trash can, and missed.

It's never been easy to be Helen Nilsson's twin. Since day one, she's been better than me at just about everything, save the most boring kinds of schoolwork. Sometimes people call us "the Nilsson Twins," but just as often they call us "the Helen Twins." I was glad Helen didn't know I had a crush on her best friend. Because she would give me such grief. Make fun of me for sitting around thinking about it instead of doing something.

The Fall Formal was coming up quick. Boys started asking girls during the first week of class, I'd heard. And I knew I wouldn't be the only guy who thought Nicki was cute. Someone would ask her if I didn't. And what made my procrastination seem even worse, I had the best op portunity of all, since she was my sister's friend and I saw her all the time.

I glanced at the wall clock, then went to the TV and turned it on. My favorite show, *The Dead of Night*, was on soon. I don't know if you know that show, but it was a half-hour-long weekly series where strange things happened to people, sometimes terrifying things. Occasionally it was so scary I couldn't sleep afterward, and yet I never missed an episode.

The picture tube started warming up, which takes about a minute, the little dot at the center appearing first, and growing brighter before finally engulfing the whole screen. A science book I read a while ago talked about the Big Bang, which supposedly created everything. I imagine it being like a TV turning on — that little dot heating up and then, *whammo*, exploding into the show of the universe.

As I waited, I remembered those books we'd taken, in my rucksack. I fetched them from the kitchen, but before I could begin looking through them, the sound came up on the TV and the screen filled. *The Dead of Night* was just starting, with its creepy intro: "You're walking down a roadway in the forest, toward the graveyard, lost . . . in . . . *the dead of night!*"

The episode this time was about a black man in the South who was taking a city bus really late, and it was just him and the driver, who was white. They got to talking, and the driver told the black guy he shouldn't fight for civil rights, and should just accept the way things were. Then, when the bus stopped and the doors opened, the white guy stepped out, as if he was the passenger, and the black guy was suddenly the driver. Outside, everyone on the street was black. And there was segregation everywhere, but against white people—a drinking fountain labeled "Blacks Only," and a hotel with a sign saying "Whites Use Service Entrance," and other stuff. The white guy, in the end, was chased by a pickup truck full of drunk black guys. He disappeared down the road . . . into . . . the dead of night.

I knew from school that the South was segregated, almost everywhere. Buses, restaurants, schools, everything. That's why black people were coming in a few days to Washington D.C. for a big protest march. Here in Iowa, though, there wasn't so much segregation like in the South. There was in a few places, like some stores, or funeral homes, but not restaurants, buses, or schools. Not most places. There were hardly any black people to segregate from, anyway. I'd only seen a few in my whole life.

So, this episode of the show wasn't particularly interesting to me. I preferred the ones where there was a deal with the devil, or space aliens. I really liked space aliens, and space in general.

Last year President Kennedy started the Apollo project, to send a person to the moon. And after that maybe farther, to Mars, or even another star. Whenever someone asked me what I wanted to be when I grew up, I said, "An astronaut."

Thinking about space reminded me of the books from the campsite, and I picked up the top one, *Airman Crusader Versus the Centipede King*. I opened the worn paper cover and started reading.

"Airman Crusader, greatest of all airmen, strode forward, his pure white cap shining in the sun . . ." the story began.

I read *Airman Crusader Versus the Centipede King* in one sitting. It was great. Airman Crusader and his fellow airmen hear about this secret potion that could make a person live forever. It was hidden on the planet of the centipede creatures, who were these disgusting bugs that drooled green poison from black fangs. The airmen decided they should steal the potion—that the centipedes shouldn't be immortal, because they were evil. It would be better if the airmen were immortal, because they were the good guys. So they went to the centipede planet and broke into the centipede city, which was tunnels underground. The airmen killed the centipedes until they reached the throne room. They interrogated the king, who was as big as a building, and it turned out the centipedes didn't have the potion—it had already been stolen by the bat creatures, who lived in a totally different part of the galaxy.

Then the centipede king tried to stab Airman Crusader with his poison tail, but Crusader was quick and shot the king with a blaster. A big wave of goo squirted out of the massive king, which carried all of the airmen back to the surface. Then they flew their spaceship home.

"Will Airman Crusader find the potion of immortality?" the narrator asked at the end. "Read *Airman Crusader Versus the Bat Creatures* to find out!"

I wanted to read it immediately, but first I went to the kitchen, where the chili was simmering. In my mind the book played over, and I imagined that I was Airman Crusader, battling the evil and repulsive centipede creatures. As I divided the chili into servings, I imagined myself firing my blaster into the legion hordes of centipedes, bug legs flying everywhere. I put some of the chili in the fridge for Mom and Dad, some into a bowl for myself, and some in a Tupperware container for Helen, for whenever she got back from whatever she was doing (primarily avoiding cooking this chili).

Since I was getting up early tomorrow for the first day of school, I decided to turn in and read awhile in bed. I carried the stack of paperbacks with me upstairs and put it on my bed. Then I changed into my pajamas, still imagining that I was fighting the inhuman hordes of centipedes, and brushed my teeth.

Not much to say about my bedroom, which is pretty uninteresting. Aside from my bed there's a linoleum-topped desk, a bookshelf, and a closet with a full-length mirror on the door. I asked for my own record player for my birthday this year, but they're expensive and I didn't get one.

If my room is full of anything at this time of year,

it's heat. Upstairs is always hotter than downstairs. I was sweating and I opened my window wide, and some slightly cooler air came in smelling of cedar (we have cedar shakes on the roof). I got into bed with just the sheet over me. It had been like this almost all summer, and I was more or less used to it.

I turned on my reading light and moved the stack of books to my bedside table. I also turned on my radio (which is what I got for my birthday instead of the record player). The fuzzy music came on and I kept the volume low — I knew just how low it had to be to not annoy anyone. I like listening to the radio as I fall asleep. Elvis had a new song out called "Are You Lonesome Tonight?" that the station DJs sometimes played just before KRW went off the air. At the moment, "Rock Around the Clock" was playing.

My eye throbbed painfully, reminding me of the fight, and in my mind's eye I saw Carl looming up, his giant fist plunging at me.

It hadn't always been like this with him. He used to be kind of nice.

I'd known Carl and Alan for about four years, ever since they moved to Farro. They'd sort of crash-landed in the mobile home up the road after their dad washed out of the major leagues. Carl was a freshman at the high school, and he started on the varsity team. Everyone in town who had even a passing interest in baseball knew about the Dunns, and about their dad Elmore in particular, who was kind of famous for having been a Native American pitcher.

Helen and I biked past their place about a week after they moved in (riding the bikes we had then, mine blue and hers pink) to find Carl standing in the field out front, plotting a baseball diamond.

He asked if we'd help him. I was a little wary, Carl being a stranger and older than us, and big. But he wasn't mean then. He seemed happy for the help. Together we blocked out the diamond, and Carl hammered stakes with string running between to define the baselines until he could lime them. Then he let us take a few swings with his beat-up old Louisville Slugger.

"Kid, I hope you got interests outside baseball," he said to me, laughing after I missed his second easy pitch.

Thinking back on that day now, I puzzled over Carl. He'd gotten meaner slowly, at first. I remembered one summer where he never spoke, just glared at things. The following year, Alan said Carl wasn't doing well in school, and was maybe going to get kicked off the baseball team.

Then he started shoving us around. Eventually, I don't know exactly when, I became afraid of him. I avoided him, and so did other kids. This summer was the worst. Bullying became a mission for Carl, like a new sport that had replaced baseball.

"Henry," Carl had said that first day, smiling after I struck out on his slow tosses, "you should meet my younger brother. I think you're the same age." Then he'd yelled back toward the house, "Hey, Alan, are you in there? There's a kid out here you should be friends with." That distant voice echoed in my mind as I looked at the covers of the Airman Crusader books, with their lightning-bolt titles:

Airman Crusader Versus the Bat Creatures, Airman Crusader Versus the Rats, Airman Crusader Versus the Venusians, Airman Crusader Versus the Airmen . . .

Then I reached the last volume in the stack, and paused. The cover didn't feature lightning bolts, aliens, or laser blasts. It was just black, no illustration at all, only a title like on a textbook: *Subtle Travel and the Subtle Self.* There were two authors. One was A. Møller, who wrote the Airman Crusader books, and the second was J. Brody.

It was as dog-eared as the rest of the paperbacks, just as grimy and with cracks along the spine. I turned it over to see what the summary said on the back, but there wasn't anything. The back was blank too, without even a price listed.

I opened to the first page.

> **CHAPTER ONE**
> **You think you are one person in one body, but that is a fault of perception. In fact, you are one person in two bodies. Your first body: weight, mass, matter. Your second body: weightless, massless, flow—the subtle form. One body upon the other, within the other, each the shadow of the other. The subtle sleeps and wakes with and within the physical, or so it has been. Now learn: The physical sleeps, the subtle wakes! The physical lies still, the subtle walks! This is the art we teach.**

I barely noticed Helen's footsteps on the stairs as she came up to the second floor and got ready for bed. It must have been pretty late. She brushed her teeth, and I dimly heard her in the hall. Then she appeared in my open doorway. "G'night, Henry," she said.

"G'night," I answered, not even looking up.

"Thanks for the chili," she said.

"Yup," I replied, still reading.

"School tomorrow," said Helen. "We're junior high kids now."

"Uh-huh," I agreed.

Helen realized that she would get nothing out of me. She padded off to her room, and I heard her door click shut.

I'd never been more absorbed in a book. I was even a little scared. It didn't seem like a story. It seemed like it was describing something real — that a person could step right out of their body while their body was sleeping. You'd be yourself, but invisible. This was called "subtle travel." The part of you that did the walking, your second body, was called "the subtle form."

Lie atop the covers, one arm up as illustrated in fig. 1, index finger extended. Recite the nine-number series, and repeat: 1, 1, 2, 3, 5, 8, 13, 21, 34. When you continue beyond these digits, you will be awake to the subtle plane. Enter the paralysis. Using your eyes, rock yourself from your sleeping body. Now you are free. Walk without fear.

I didn't understand everything. What did it mean to recite beyond the nine digits? What was the paralysis? How do you rock yourself with your eyes? It seemed like half instructions and half poetry.

I put the book aside, and looked at the clock. It was after midnight — way later than I should have been up.

As the book had instructed, I lay down and propped my arm with a pillow so my forearm was sticking up, my hand in the air. It wasn't very comfortable.

I closed my eyes and started reciting the numbers, silently: "1, 1, 2, 3, 5, 8, 13, 21, 34." When I reached the end, I began again. Pretty soon, probably because it was so late, I got sleepy. I started losing track, but whenever I did I just returned to the beginning. "1, 1, 2, 3, 5, 8 . . . 13 . . ." I started over: "1, 1, 2, 3, 5 . . ." Start over. "1, 1, 2, 3 . . ." I was drifting off quickly, wobbling between a waking state and dreaming. And to my surprise, I found myself in the middle of saying, "55 . . . 89 . . ." Where did those numbers come from? I was really starting to lose my place. I began once again and tried to be careful as I went up, but my brain was going all strange. And this time when I reached 34, I didn't feel like I needed to start over. It was kind of like I'd hiked to the lip of a hill, and when I got to the top I just walked right up into the air: 55, 89,

144, 233, 377, 610, 987, 1597, 2584, 4181, 6765, 10946, 17711, 28657, 46368, 75025 . . .

I kept concentrating, and the numbers showed no sign of stopping: 121393, 196418, 317811, 514229, 832040, 1346269, 2178309, 3524578, 5702887, 9227465, 14930352, 24157817, 39088169 . . .

I opened my eyes. I guessed I'd awakened. The numbers were gone. The radio had roused me, I thought—"Are You Lonesome Tonight?" was playing. I lay there and listened to it. Lots of people considered it a romantic song, but I thought it was creepy. In the lyrics, Elvis describes this empty house, with an empty parlor and empty chairs, like a ghost story.

As he sang, I decided to sit up, because it was kind of getting to me, my own house being queer and quiet and dark like the one where he was. But when I tried, I couldn't. I told myself, "Sit up," but nothing moved except my eyes, which jerked left and right as I struggled. I felt a sudden rush of fear as the song ended, and I dimly heard on the radio, "This is KRW, signing off for the end of our broadcast day." A burst of static came over the speakers, then silence, and I finally remembered—the book had described this state. This was "the paralysis."

My brain was groggy. What was I supposed to do? After the numbers, I'd wake up and find myself stuck—my subtle form attached to my physical body like a lining zipped into a coat. Then it came to me. "Using your eyes, rock yourself . . ."

It made sense. I started rocking my eyeballs back and forth, looking left, then right, then left, then right. A momentum began to build. My whole self sloshed like water in a tub, left, right, left, right—

And I spilled out of myself. That's the only way I can describe it. My line of sight peeled down the walls in one quick tip, and next thing I knew I was staring at the carpet. I was on the floor.

I stood, a little dizzy. I turned around and looked down at my bed.

There I was, sleeping in it.

CHAPTER 4

LOOKING DOWN AT MYSELF I saw that my arm, which I'd balanced upright, was lying on my chest. When it fell, that's what broke through the paralysis, I guessed. "Incredible," I whispered. My voice sounded strange, close, like in a telephone booth. It didn't bounce off the walls like a normal voice. Because it wasn't normal. It was . . . a subtle voice.

My body was sleeping peacefully. I could see the black eye starting up where Carl had punched me. And my ears really did stick out, maybe more now than ever. I did not look like someone's dance date, but this wasn't the time to dwell on it.

Scanning the rest of my room, I realized my sense of sight was altered. I could tell the room was dark—pitch dark—but I could still see. It looked to me like someone had come in and painted everything black and left the lights on. My desk, instead of being brown and green, was black. My walls, instead of being off-white, were black.

The top blanket of my bed, instead of being blue and red, was black.

Also, snow. Yes, it appeared to be snowing in here, indoors, in the middle of summer. There were flakes everywhere, lofting around in little gusts. Sometimes they'd stick to one another, or break apart, everything happening slow and graceful. Unlike the rest of the black room, the flakes were different colors — some dark blue, others red or green or brown. Some landed on me as I watched, soaked into my clothes, and disappeared. A few flakes whirled out through my bedroom window and disappeared outside. I wondered if it was snowing there too, and I went to the sill and leaned out to see.

No sooner had I taken a glance, though, than a voice from below shouted up at me angrily, "I knew it was you, you little thief!"

I looked down on the front yard and driveway. Someone was there — and not just any someone. This was perhaps the very last person in the whole world I'd want yelling at me in the middle of the night: Carl Dunn. He was standing on the front walk.

There's something else I should mention. I'm not exactly sure how to put it aside from saying that Carl, well, he wasn't looking quite his normal self. I mean, he did look like who he was, with his big arms, pimply face, and dark tan from a long summer. I knew him without a doubt. He was even wearing the same clothes as earlier—a white T-shirt and blue jeans. The strange thing wasn't any of that.

The thing was . . . his head was on fire.

And not just a little. It was massively on fire, a giant blaze with bright whitish flames leaping up and a huge column of cottony smoke billowing out.

I rubbed my eyes, but the problem wasn't with my sight. The flames jetted from where Carl's hair should have been, and the smoke chugged like from a train on a mountain ascent.

Now, I can say with some certainty that if I ever happened to find my own head on fire, I would prioritize putting it out. I mean, no matter what else was going on, I'd do that first. And if I saw someone nearby, I'd say something to them like, "Help me," or maybe "Please help me" if they looked reluctant. I would not say what Carl said next, which was, "Come down here, you little thief, or I'm coming up."

I stared in speechless amazement.

"Jump," said Carl, gesturing as if he thought I'd really take a leap from the second floor.

I hadn't thought that I could be any more scared of Carl Dunn than I already was, but seeing the flames billowing up from him, and him not caring one way or the other about it, he seemed like some kind of supernatural being. My knees were knocking together, I was so terrified. I took him at his word that he'd come up if I didn't go down, so I said, my voice quivering, "I'll be right there."

I stepped back from the window and walked into the hall, which was not lit. It should have been pitch dark, but I could still see perfectly, everything colored black.

I descended the stairs to the entryway. The wall clock read one fifteen. Mom and Dad wouldn't be home for an hour. "And this is a dream," I told myself. But it kept seeming not like a dream.

I reached to open the front door, and to my surprise my hand passed right through the knob. I tried again, same result. As if I was a ghost. Well, if there was one thing I knew about ghosts, it was that they weren't stopped by doors.

I stepped forward, flinching a little when I was about to hit. Then my nose just went right through. Have you ever spent time in the middle of a door? It smells of sawdust and sap in there, and the wood grain and layers of glue are thin as pages. Doors are kind of like books.

Quick as anything I was through, standing outside.

Carl was right there, by the driveway. Something still billowed from his flaming head, but now that I was closer I saw it wasn't smoke. It was snowflakes. They weren't all different colors like the ones in my room, but almost all white, like real snow. They poured out of the flames, flying up in the exact opposite direction of normal snow. "Carl, why are you . . . ?" I said.

"Shut up," he replied. He stepped toward me and I cowered back, but he didn't hit me. "You stole Abe's books," he said. "I'm gonna tell him, and you'll be sorry."

I knew he was talking about the books at the campsite, and I didn't say anything in my own defense. I just stood there shaking.

"But it doesn't matter," said Carl. His voice sounded clipped, and I noticed, which I had not expected, that he seemed nervous.

"Carl," I said, "are you okay?" I glanced significantly up at the fire.

Carl smiled, and gestured at the flames. "See how pure it is?" he said. He seemed pleased about this, bragging as you might about a good grade. I had no idea what he meant, but before I could ask anything, his demeanor changed. He started and spun around, like he'd heard something behind him. He peered across the street into the scrub and trees there, and stammered, "Did you hear that?"

"I didn't hear anything," I said.

"There's a ghost out there."

I was so confused by everything he was saying, all I could do was stand there stupidly.

"I saw his dead body," said Carl. "We set traps, but he snuck past them. Now we don't know where he is."

"Carl, Alan's worried about you," I said.

He stepped close to me, his chest level with my eyeballs. I looked away, glancing over toward the front porch. The light there was burned out, leaving a dark area where I could clearly see the white snowflakes drifting. I waited for Carl's blow, but it didn't come. He was looking over at the flakes too. "I'm going underground," he said, quietly.

Then he stepped back and turned to leave, as if he'd forgotten all about me, which normally I'd take as a stroke of incredible luck. But I remembered how Alan said Carl had done a poor job of hiding his own diary—almost like he wanted it found. And now here he was, accusing me of being a thief and then walking away. "Carl, wait," I said. "Do you need help?"

For a second I thought he'd give me a real answer, but then the light in his eyes hardened. "I'm gonna live forever," he said, and he continued off into the darkness. Within seconds, all that remained of him was a vanishing trail of snowflakes.

CHAPTER 5

MY ALARM WENT OFF at six a.m. I awakened thinking not about the very strange dream I'd had, but about how much my face hurt. I put one hand up to my cheek. The bulge there felt like a baby bird.

I went to my closet-door mirror and hesitantly took my hand away. Oh no, I thought. Not on the first day of junior high . . .

Downstairs, Helen was already up. She was wearing one of her regular school dresses, strange to see after a summer of jeans. She'd cooked eggs for us both, which was a pleasant surprise—but she was more surprised than I was when I walked in. "Henry, what a shiner!" she exclaimed. "Does it hurt?"

"Yes." I sat glumly at the table. There was a scrap of paper in the middle, a note left by Mom and Dad when they got in earlier. As I reached for it, Helen said, "I took care of that. The porch light burned out."

And I remembered—in my dream, noticing the burned-out light.

"Also," Helen added, "we're in trouble."

I didn't think about the trouble. I was too busy with the porch light. I would not have known that light was burned out, unless maybe I really had walked through the front door, like a ghost, and seen Carl . . .

Distractedly, I scanned the rest of the note. "Come straight home after school," it read, in Mom's hand. "We need to talk about fighting."

"Oh boy," I said.

"It wasn't our fault!" said Helen as she slid an egg onto a plate for me.

We were out the front door soon after, my schoolbooks and hers crammed into my rucksack. We pedaled to Nicki's house. I wasn't saying much, and I'm sure Helen assumed it was because I was worried about being in trouble, or about having a black eye on the first day of school. Which I was, both. But I was also remembering Carl's head, belching snowflakes out of weird flames.

Nicki's house looked similar to ours, two stories with a

low fence around. She was outside on her bike, wearing a blue jacket and a brown corduroy skirt, which was about the cutest outfit ever.

"Hi, Nicki," I said.

She rode past me holding out one hand for a high-five, but I missed it.

"That is some kind of black eye, Henry," she said.

I felt my ears turning red.

We headed up the highway. A couple of cars passed us and honked—friends getting rides from their parents.

When we were almost at the school, Alan caught up to us on his rickety bike.

I rode toward him and held up a high-five, but he didn't try to hit it. I leered at him comically out of my swollen black eye, and saw he was looking very serious. "Everything okay?" I asked.

"Carl didn't come home last night," he said.

"Never?" said Helen.

"You mean, he's going to miss school?" said Nicki. She was imagining, I think, how her own strict parents would react if she missed the first day, or any day, for that matter. School was very important at her house.

"Does your dad know?" Helen asked.

"I doubt it," said Alan. "He's sleeping."

"You guys," I said, suddenly intent. "I have . . . something . . ." I paused as we reached the school parking lot. "I'll tell you in homeroom," I said.

Johnson Junior High was big, a real school, not a rinky-dink elementary. At the front was a pair of giant double doors, propped open as kids poured through. The portal transformed us from sixth graders into seventh graders. From grade schoolers into junior high students.

I'm sure we looked wide-eyed as we surveyed the big halls. Well, one of my eyes was wide-eyed. The other was narrow as a coin slot.

Everything here was bigger than in elementary school, and more serious. There were no silly pieces of wall art made by kindergartners. The walls had lockers, and flyers were stuck to a few boards with official-looking announcements. I was glad to be with my sister and friends.

"This place is big," I said.

"Naw," said Helen.

We found our room and entered.

It was arranged pretty casually. I'd expected rows of somber gray desks, but instead there were tables and chairs in little groups all through the room. It was filling with kids, about half of whom I knew, talking with one another about what they'd been up to during the summer.

As we headed toward a table at the back I had to fend off some jibes about my eye. Someone called me Quasimodo, which I didn't get. Someone asked Helen if she'd beaten me up. "If it was me, they'd both be black," she said.

The final bell rang and the teacher, Mr. McTavish, closed the door. McTavish was a huge guy. He must have been six foot four, and wide, with square shoulders like a piano bench. He had a black beard that covered his whole neck, and he wore a pair of black horn-rimmed glasses. I knew who he was, because he was the coach of the school's baseball team and Alan had talked about him. It was funny to see him, though — he looked built for football, not baseball. Alan said McTavish was friends with Coach Wilson, the head coach at Johnson High School.

"Welcome, seventh graders," said McTavish. His voice was one of those big instruments engineered to silence classrooms instantly. He got out his roll sheet and started calling names. About halfway through he said, "Helen Nilsson," and then, "Henry Nilsson." (Not only is Helen twenty minutes older than me, but her name is ahead of mine alphabetically.)

"We call him One-eye Nilsson, Mr. McTavish," said someone, and the class laughed.

I froze. First day. I had to make a decent showing here. "They don't call me that," I said loudly. "They call me . . . um . . ." I had to think of a better nickname, fast. But I am not fast. I sat there tongue-tied and the moment was lost.

McTavish finished roll, then read the morning announcements. The last was, "The School Spirit Committee would like to remind you that the all-school Fall Formal will occur two weeks from today. Remember, boys, it's never too early to ask your sweetheart."

McTavish said he'd give us a few more minutes to socialize, then went behind his desk. The room grew loud again as summer stories were resumed.

"Henry, what were you going to tell us?" said Helen.

I didn't reply at first, sunk as I was in a sudden quicksand of fear about asking my sweetheart to the dance. She was sitting right across from me, long black hair shining in the fluorescent lights, and slim, bare forearms resting on the tabletop. I'd just been commanded to ask her. I was staring, and it seemed like maybe she was staring back . . .

"Attention, Apollo spacecraft," Helen said, and whacked me on the side of the head. "This is Mission Control."

Moment lost. I reached to the back of my chair, where I'd slung my rucksack, and pulled out *Subtle Travel and the Subtle Self.* "You guys aren't going to believe this," I said, as I laid it on the table. And I told it all, just as it had happened.

"Henry, are you serious?" said Alan, when I'd finished.

"And the porch light?" said Nicki. "You're sure you saw it like that?"

"Maybe you saw it was burned out earlier, Henry, but didn't realize you had," said Helen. Actually, this kind of made sense, which deflated me a little.

Helen took the book, opened it, and flipped through the first few pages. "Henry, remember that dead dog you thought was in the basement?" she asked.

"I remember," I said, deflating even more. Once I thought I saw a dead dog in our basement, and got Mom to go down looking for it. But there was no dead dog. The dead dog was a dream.

"Still, this is pretty strange," said Nicki, taking the

book from Helen and flipping to the opening, where she began to read.

"And if it does have something to do with Carl," said Alan, "I want to know more."

"Let's all memorize these numbers you learned, Henry," said Nicki.

"Yeah," said Helen, "what's the worst that could happen?"

"Well," I said, realistically, "we don't really know."

Nicki still had the book, and furrowed her brow as she struggled through the strange writing. "Here's a section titled "The Invulnerable Subtle Form." Doesn't *invulnerable* mean—"

"Invincible?" said Helen, leaning over.

Then, from the front of the room, McTavish's voice called out: "Alan Dunn, could I see you up here for a moment?"

Alan looked at us nervously. "It's got to be about Carl," he said.

"I'll go with you," I offered.

We approached together. "Have a seat, Alan," said McTavish. He turned to me. "You're Henry Nilsson, is that right?"

"Yes, sir," I said.

"Your eye looks terrible, son."

"It's okay," I said. "It's just embarrassing."

McTavish put his gigantic forearms on the desk, big as badgers. "Alan, we got a call from the high school that your brother is absent. They've tried unsuccessfully to reach your father. So I wanted to check with you."

"He didn't come home last night," said Alan. "I heard he missed practice. But I don't know any more than that."

This was a situation unlike any I'd been in before. I knew something that might be important, but I couldn't just say, 'I saw Carl last night in a dream and his head was on fire.' So I stood there and looked uncomfortable.

"How long has he been gone?" asked McTavish.

"Since yesterday afternoon," said Alan.

"That's when I last saw him, too," I said. I gestured to my eye.

"Carl did that?" said McTavish. "Alan, have you talked to your father about this?"

"Er, no, not yet," said Alan.

"Well, do so. And if you haven't seen Carl by this evening, you must report it to the police."

"Yes, sir," said Alan.

"Alan, I know he's been struggling," said McTavish. "I want to help if I can."

"Thank you, sir," said Alan.

I could tell none of this was making Alan feel any better.

CHAPTER 6

DURING LUNCH the four of us got together to pore over the book some more. We carefully studied the instructions in chapter one.

"Henry, what's this part about paralysis?" said Nicki.

"It scared me at first," I said. "You wake up, and it's like you're trapped in your own body. But you can still move your eyes — see here, where it says 'Using your eyes . . .'"

We went over it all. And we practiced the numbers. Since I already knew them, I tested my friends, like we were drilling for a math quiz. I'm sure we looked pretty strange huddled at our table in the cafeteria chanting, "1! 1! 2! 3! 5! 8!"

Helen was the last to master it. I could tell it was hard for her, and I also think it bugged her to have me teaching her something.

"Not 12 — 13," I corrected, after she made the same mistake twice.

"What does it matter?" said Helen, throwing up her hands.

"Come on, Helen," said Nicki. "Let's start again. I still need to work on it too. 1, 1, 2, 3 . . ."

Of course, we didn't know for sure if my experience had been real, and sitting in the sweaty, noisy cafeteria with the afternoon sun blasting in through the windows, I felt doubtful. Maybe it was a coincidence that the porch light had been out. Maybe I'd noticed it earlier without realizing it, as Helen said.

After school the four of us rode together for a few blocks on the way home. "Alan, I hope Carl's back," I said as we reached Alan's turnoff.

"I bet he'll be there," said Helen.

"I'll let you guys know," said Alan, "tonight, when I see you . . . in our dreams!" He rode away laughing, but I could tell he was worried.

Helen, Nicki, and I continued along. My shirt sagged on me as we wove our bikes from one side of the road to the other, hunting for the shade of some of the bigger trees. When we reached Nicki's turnoff, Helen said, "See you tonight, hopefully."

"1, 1, 2, 3, 5, 8," said Nicki.

I didn't really look at her as she left us—I saw a glint of fender, a bend of elbow, and she was gone. Helen and I kept riding, not speaking, both of us thinking about the unavoidable fact that we were in trouble, and that Mom and Dad would be there when we got home, waiting to lecture us.

"It wasn't our fault," said Helen.

"Don't say that," I said. "It makes it seem like it was."

"Bet you wish you were on the Apollo mission right now," said Helen with a rueful grin.

I'd never thought of that before, but it was true: being an astronaut was potentially a great way to escape from your parents.

We reached home and parked our bikes on the side. I saw the afternoon paper at the foot of the steps, picked it up, and worked out the creases for Dad.

Helen, who normally storms in, sometimes even opening the screen door with her head, hung back and let me lead the way. The kitchen was empty. I placed the paper on the table, and heard Mom talking to Dad in the living room. "Thomas," she said, "did you read that Joseph, from Rotary Club, passed away on Saturday? It's so sad. I wonder how his wife is doing."

As was often the case, Mom was reading yesterday's paper while Dad read today's. Papers had a regular route through our house that started with Dad, passed through Mom, and ended with Helen or me reading the comics before we threw the whole thing out.

We entered the living room, and there were Mom and Dad, sitting next to each other, reading. I cleared my throat, and both newspapers lowered. Dad's crewcut appeared, and his tired blue eyes.

Mom was also blond, like Dad, though her hair was long and tied back in a ponytail. She had a wide forehead, and blue eyes that also looked tired.

It seemed as if Dad was going to get the lecture started. I turned to him, and he paused as he mentally arranged his opening statement. But he didn't have a chance to deliver it, because something else happened—Mom saw my black eye.

She dropped her paper, leaped to her feet, and ran to me saying, "Henry, my god!" She grabbed me and started inspecting my eye, taking my head in both hands and peering deep, maybe to see if I was still in there. "Who did this to you, Henry?" she asked.

"Carl," I said. There was no use denying it, since I'd already told Dad.

"Carl Dunn," Mom snarled. Every parent in town knew Carl from the injuries he'd given their kids, especially this past summer. She took a deep breath and tried to calm herself. "I don't want you to have anything more to do with that family, Henry," she said.

I gulped. Mom was so angry that she'd reached what Helen and I called "Pronouncement Level," which almost never happened—a high degree of rage in which she'd make some sweeping proclamation. To be forbidden from seeing my best friend . . . my mind leaped, trying to figure a way out. But at Pronouncement Level there wasn't room for discussion. The best strategy was to let things quiet down and come back to it later.

"Your mother and I have already talked about this," said Dad. "You aren't going to like it, either of you, but it's for the best. You are both grounded immediately, for fighting. We especially don't want you seeing the Dunns."

"But, Dad," I whined, "Alan isn't—"

"That's our decision," said Dad, interrupting me. Dad

hated whining, and I knew he did, but I was really up-set. Sometimes when you're really upset, you whine even though it works against you.

"While you're grounded," Dad continued, "you aren't to see the Chens, either. You're not to go over to their house. You're not to socialize after school."

"What?" said Helen, and I think she really did imagine she'd misheard.

"Dis-missed," said Dad. He shook the paper, preparing to go back to it. But Helen and I could not let this go — it was too colossally unfair.

"But why, Dad?" I said. "What did Nicki do?"

"You're too young to understand," said Dad.

"What are we too young to understand?" said Helen, her voice shaking.

Dad didn't reply. He raised the paper and his face disappeared behind it.

I could almost understand about the Dunns. Obviously, it was a good idea for us to avoid Carl. Even I could get behind that. And people seemed to dislike Mr. Dunn, too — I'd heard parents talking about him, calling him a drunk and stuff. But the Chens? It made no sense.

Our cause was lost for now, though. I urged Helen with my eyes to just nod and leave the room with me. But

Helen is not that kind of person. When she saw I'd given up, she shouted, "It wasn't even our fault! You two are out of your minds!"

Then — and I'd never seen her do something quite like this before — she attacked. She lunged forward, grabbed the newspaper out of Dad's hands, and tore it in half, throwing the remnants over her shoulder as she raced from the room and out of the house. She was pedaling her bike away by the time the kitchen screen door slapped shut behind her.

CHAPTER 7

THAT EVENING I MADE mulligan stew for Mom and Dad. I was mad at them, sure, but they still needed dinner. Once it was cooked, cooled, and in the fridge, Helen came home. I bet she'd ridden twenty miles to boil off her anger.

She sat at the kitchen table. I put out bowls for us, and we ate silently. After, Helen washed the dishes and we went upstairs to brush our teeth.

"Henry," she said, "what are they thinking? Why?" She was sincerely grieved, and I felt just the same. "They didn't even let us explain."

"I think they're worried about other stuff," I said. "Work, the strike, Dad getting laid off. They want to think about their own problems, not ours."

"It's awful," said Helen.

"You don't have to tell me," I said, "but there's something they don't know about, right?"

"What's that?" said Helen, as she kept brushing. Helen did not fool around about tooth brushing. She always seemed intent on sanding her teeth right down to the gums.

"1, 1, 2, 3, 5, 8, 13, 21, 34," I recited.

Helen stared down into the sink.

I should mention that I know my sister pretty well. I mean, I'm her twin. She's got a temper, sure, but grabbing the paper from Dad—that was too much, even for her. There was something else going on.

"What is it, Helen?" I said.

She rinsed out her mouth and then said, quoting the morning announcement, "Boys, it's never too early to invite your sweetheart to the Fall Formal."

"What do you mean?" I asked, my voice cracking because I thought she'd figured out my crush on Nicki. Maybe she even knew something. That Nicki wasn't interested. Or was going with someone else. Or . . .

"I just wonder if anyone will ask me," she said with a sigh.

"Eh?" I replied. Helen wanted to go to the dance? I flashed for a second to imagining her in a frilly dress.

"It's just . . . that . . ." she said. I'd never seen her at such a loss. She put her hands heavily on either side of the sink. "I want Alan to ask me," she said.

"Alan . . . Alan Dunn?" I said.

"Yes, Alan Dunn," said Helen, "who we are now forbidden to see."

I was stupefied. Helen and Alan. It had never crossed my mind. "How . . . long . . . ?" I said.

"He hasn't mentioned anything to you, has he?" she said.

Now I was the one at a loss, wondering if this would be a good moment to mention my own crush. But as usual, the opportunity passed before I figured out what to do. Then Helen got angry and shouted, "Why do the guys always have to ask? Why can't girls ask? It's stupid!" This last was as if I were responsible for it.

"Well, maybe I could—" I began.

"No, don't do anything," said Helen, and she stomped out and down the hall to her room, slamming the door behind her.

My mind was swimming. Helen and Alan! Their names kind of rhymed. I smiled. It was gratifying to see my sister so wound up about a problem she couldn't solve. For a change.

Once in my room, I arranged things again according to the book's instructions. I lay atop the sheets and balanced my arm upright with a pillow. It was hot again, and I was sweating.

I focused my attention and began to count silently: 1, 1, 2, 3, 5, 8, 13 . . .

But my thoughts were reluctant to stay on task. They got distracted by images from the day, like the moment during roll call when I'd failed to invent a better nickname for myself than "One-eye Nilsson." I felt the embarrassment all over again.

The thoughts wouldn't leave me. I got out of bed, went to my desk, found paper and pencil, and started writing. It took me awhile, but eventually I thought of Eightball, which was pretty good. Then the ideas came faster: TKO, Evil Eye, Perry Scope.

I folded the paper and put it in my wallet, just in case the issue came up again.

I returned to bed.

1, 1, 2, 3, 5, 8, 13 . . .

Eventually, the numbers kept going up, like a kite lifting, and entered the paralysis. I opened my eyes and, just as I had the night before, found myself staring up at the ceiling, unable to move.

But then things stopped being identical to the previous night. From nearby me, a man's voice suddenly spoke.

"Hello there, young man," it said. If I hadn't been paralyzed, I'd have jumped to my feet. As it was, I blinked furiously and rolled my eyes around in my skull.

The voice had come from my left. It was low, a little raspy. It had a friendly tone to it, but I was not put at ease. After all, this person had come into my bedroom without permission, and I'd learned from a lifetime of TV shows and school assemblies that such people are not generally well-intentioned.

Out of the corner of my eye, I could see a vague form standing by my bed, a man of average build, wearing what looked like pajamas—the kind with the vertical blue stripes—and a white hat of some kind, which shone bright in my mostly black room.

I started rocking my eyes quickly, hoping to shake myself out of my body, but the man said, "That won't work if you rush it. Just be still for a moment, son. No harm will come. I have a question to ask you."

I surprised myself by replying—apparently my mouth could work as well as my eyes. "Who are you?" I said.

"Next time we meet, you can question me," said the man, "but tonight I'm going to question you, Henry." I didn't know when these turns had been established, but I didn't challenge him. My blood ran cold when he said my name. How did he know me? "You've been awake in the subtle world for at least a night, so tell me honestly, while you've been traveling, have you met a violinist?"

I'm not sure what question I was expecting, but that was definitely not it. It was so strange, I thought I must have misheard him. "Excuse me?" I asked.

"A violinist," the man repeated. "A player of the violin. Do you know what a violin is? This man is very dangerous. He is a criminal, and I'm looking for him. I'm asking for your help."

"No," I said. "I haven't met any . . . violinists."

"He's clever," said the man. "Clever and treacherous. If you see him, I hope you'll let me know."

"How do I do that?" I said.

The man didn't answer. He had vanished.

I hadn't ever known a person to disappear into thin air before, and I didn't like it. I rolled my eyes all around in my head and listened carefully. . . but he really was gone. Of course, if someone can disappear, it follows that they can reappear, and I waited for a sudden voice to come out of the shadows. Eventually, though, as I watched the colorful snowflakes lob through the air above me, I calmed down enough to start rocking my eyes properly, and soon I managed to break through the paralysis and roll out of myself.

I stood and immediately surveyed the room, verifying that I was alone. On my bed, my body slept peacefully. My shiner was still visible, even in the dark. "They call me Bull's Eye," I whispered.

"Henry," said a voice from behind.

I jumped, and turned to find Helen standing in my doorway. When I saw her, I said the first thing that came to my mind. Shouted it, actually: "Your head is on fire!" I said.

"So's yours," Helen retorted. "Look in the closet mirror."

We both stood before it. There I was, a scrawny kid wearing blue-striped boxer shorts and a faded blue pajama top with a picture of Saturn on it. My big ears were sticking out as always. But over those ears, things were not as usual. Instead of some close-cut blond hair, my forehead disappeared into what really did look like flames, roaring bright. And out of those flames, snowflakes. But it wasn't like what I saw last night with Carl, the white steamy clouds. What came out of my flames were snowflake rainbows—all kinds of colors of flakes. I realized that I was the source of my room's snowstorm.

Helen was wearing her nightdress, which she hated— a cotton shift that reached her ankles, with flowers stitched around the hem. (Our grandmother had given it to her last Christmas.) More to the point, her flaming head was producing the same stuff as mine.

Both of us held up our hands tentatively, near the flames, which were not hot. We touched them. To me, it felt like when you stick your hand out the window of a moving car. There was no heat, just a breeze, which blew the flakes upward. I could touch the top of my head, too—it was there, inside the blaze, solid as ever. The snowflakes landed on us, melted, and sank in, but they weren't cold.

Helen, always one to hide her amazement about things, said, "Henry, your black eye's gone." Really, of all the things she could have observed right then, this seemed pretty ridiculous. But she was right. My reflection in the mirror showed no black eye. My face looked normal, as if I'd never been punched.

"So our ghosts here —" Helen began, but I interrupted her to correct: "Subtle forms."

"Right. Our subtle forms are wearing the same clothes that we're really wearing."

"Looks like," I said.

"Tomorrow, I'm going to bed in jeans then. I look like a church bell in this stupid nightgown."

"Helen," I said, "did you see a guy just now — maybe out in the hall?"

"No, nobody," said Helen. "You did?"

"Standing next to my bed," I said.

"That's creepy. Are you sure, Henry?"

"I think I'm sure," I said. "But there's lots of strange stuff going on right now."

"What did he do?"

"He asked me a question," I said, "whether I knew any violin players."

Helen eyed me quizzically, perhaps suspecting I was pulling her leg.

"I know it's odd," I said.

"Well, if it happens again, yell for me—I'm right down the hall, you know."

"I will," I said, feeling a little foolish that this hadn't occurred to me.

Helen turned from the mirror. "Henry," she said, "are you going to ask anyone to the dance?"

"Erp?" I said.

She looked at me carefully, like someone taking aim, and said, "What about Nicki?"

Then I started talking really fast. I don't know exactly what I said. Something like, "Whoa—what makes you think—no—Nicki? Who?"

"You always seem like you're trying to get up the guts," said Helen. "Honestly, Henry, it makes you look constipated."

"Oh, thanks," I replied, glancing at my sleeping form to see if my big ears were turning red.

"But I'm sure you need to think about it," said Helen, a little sarcastically.

Just then, a sound came from downstairs. We both recognized it—our parents returning from work.

"Hide," I whispered.

"But we're invisible, right?" said Helen. "Come on, let's

look." She led the way downstairs into the kitchen. The lights were on there, and the strange black hallways of upstairs gave way to what I expected to see: our nighttime kitchen, with all of its normal colors.

But what I saw was not normal.

"I can see both of them," said Helen. And so could I — that is, both Moms and both Dads. Their physical bodies and their subtle forms were right inside one another. It was one of the strangest things I'd ever seen, kind of like those nesting Russian dolls, but if the dolls were transparent.

Dad opened the fridge to retrieve the stew I'd made, and reached out his pale skinny arms, in short sleeves. Just inside those arms was another set, also in short sleeves. As Dad stepped back from the fridge, his head appeared from behind the door, with his big ears sticking out. Inside his head was his other head, which was on fire. Flakes poured out, streaming into the kitchen and going right up through the ceiling to disappear, as if there were no ceiling at all.

Dad's fire was producing some white flakes, kind of like Carl's fire had when I'd seen him the night before, but with more of a mix of other colors. As Dad placed the stew on the stove, he said to Mom, "I know he got it, Betty, because I saw him in the truck today." His voice was angry.

"Are you sure it was him?" said Mom. She was standing partly behind the kitchen cupboard door, getting out a couple of bowls. When she stepped back, I saw her, too. Her snowflakes were a little more colorful than Dad's, overall.

Amazingly, Helen was bored with this scene in about two seconds. "Let's go outside," she said.

"Hold on," I replied.

"I can't believe they gave it to him," said Dad, staring into the stew as it heated on the stove. "What kind of experience does he have?"

Mom was setting out napkins and silverware. "I don't know, Thomas," she replied. She was just letting him talk, hoping he'd wear out the topic on his own.

Dad grabbed a wooden spoon and gave the stew a brisk turn. "Maybe it's because of all that civil rights business," he said. "The utility companies see the way the wind's blowing. Immigrant rights, civil rights. It's just a smokescreen for taking jobs from qualified men."

"What are they talking about?" said Helen.

"Nicki's dad," I replied. I'd put this together just barely, but I was pretty sure. "I think he must have gotten that job Dad was applying for, with Bell Telephone."

"But why is Dad talking about immigrants? Nicki's parents were born here," said Helen.

This was true, but I knew Dad could be a little mixed up about stuff sometimes. Maybe because of what he saw in the war, or I don't know what. I'd heard him talking with Larry Petersen, the son of Carroll Petersen, who owns Petersen's Drugstore. Larry had fought in Korea too, and he and Dad talked about Korea and China and all of Asia like they were the same thing, and like everyone with brown skin was an immigrant. Nicki had pointed it out to me once.

Dad brought the stew to the table and started spooning it into the bowls while Mom sliced an orange.

"I bet it's why they grounded us from seeing Nicki," I said.

Helen's eyes went wide at this. Then she snorted angrily. "Let's get out of here," she said.

Because I already knew something about walking through closed doors, I led the way, stepping through the solid wood, smelling the pine for a split second before arriving on the front porch.

I turned to watch Helen come through. And as always she surprised me, charging out in a surprise attack I completely failed to anticipate. She shoved me with both hands and I fell, landing hard on my back on the concrete walkway. I was so startled I just lay there as she looked down at me, an expression of curiosity on her face. "You hurt?" she asked.

I sat up. I should have been hurt. I'd gone down hard. But there was no arguing it—I was fine. The breath hadn't even been knocked out of me.

"That's what I thought," said Helen. "Now push me," she said, holding out her arms.

I didn't give her a chance to retract the offer, but sprang forward instantly and gave her a tough shove. She landed on her back, as I had, laughing as she bounced. When she got up, she punched me on the nose.

"Ow!" I cried. Were this my normal body, I'd have been gushing blood. But I felt nothing beyond surprise. "We're . . . invulnerable?" I said. I'd forgotten we'd seen this in the book, but Helen probably hadn't stopped thinking about it for a second.

Now she paused and looked back at our house, her eyes going up to the second level. "I'm gonna try something," she said, and she went back inside. I waited, mull-ing over how strange it was that we could pass through the front door of the house without touching it, but could feel the stairs beneath our feet as we climbed up and down them. Why didn't we fall through the floor? I was sure there were similar mysteries lurking around every subtle corner.

Helen appeared above, in her bedroom window. She waved down to me. When I saw what she intended, I held up both hands and shouted, "Don't!"

But she did. Not only did she jump, she dove—head-first.

Head on fire, she plummeted, and slammed face down into the driveway.

I rushed toward her, but hadn't taken two steps before she leaped to her feet, threw both arms in the air, and yelled, "You gotta try it, Henry!"

"You're . . . okay?" I said, hugging her with relief.

"We are invincible," said Helen. "Does that mean nothing to you?"

Well, being invincible is one thing; watching your sister demonstrate it is another. We walked down the driveway to the road, and sat to wait for our friends.

"Nicki is a great person," said Helen, returning to our

former topic. "So are her parents. Dad has no idea about anything."

"It's the same with Alan," I said. "I mean, I know as well as anyone that Carl's a bully. And I've heard people say that Mr. Dunn's a drunk . . . but why lump Alan in? It's not fair."

Just then, we heard footsteps from up the road, in the darkness. I spotted a flame, bright in the night, with rainbows flowing up off the top.

"It's Nicki," said Helen, waving.

As her form clarified, my eyes crossed. I did not know, until that moment, what kind of clothes Nicki wore to bed. But here she was, barefoot in a red silk nightgown with embroidered cherry blossoms around the hem. She was too beautiful. I blushed, and looked at the ground.

"Your heads are on fire!" said Nicki, amazed but also laughing as she pointed at the flames.

"Don't you ever look up?" said Helen, pointing above Nicki's own head.

She looked—and laughed even harder. She danced around a little bit, and Helen joined her, and their streams of rainbow snowflakes curled and blended.

"This is unbelievable," said Nicki, still dancing—and she knew how to dance. She had told me once that her parents made her take ballroom dancing classes. Nicki played tennis, too, and volleyball, and she was good at music. Her parents signed her up for a lot of stuff. They seemed to think she should do everything, and consequently she did. She took a few quick turns now and her nightgown twirled with her, and I thought that I would never take her to the Fall Formal. Why go to a dance with a guy who can't dance?

"Also, Nicki," said Helen, "we are invulnerable."

"Someone else is coming," I said.

We fell silent as another torch appeared from up the road.

"Alan," I called out.

He was dressed in a sleeveless yellow T-shirt and gray sweatpants cut off at the knee, a much more respectable, grown-up looking outfit than my boxer shorts and Saturn shirt.

I glanced at Helen and saw her staring down at her own frilly white nightdress, frowning.

Alan waved to us as he approached. "This is incredible!" he shouted.

"We'll see if we all remember the same stuff tomorrow," said Nicki. "I mean, this could all just be a dream I'm having."

"Or me," said Helen.

"What's up with our heads?" said Alan, gesturing toward the flames.

"It was different last night, with Carl," I said.

"You guys," said Alan, suddenly serious. "My dad still hasn't seen him—nobody has."

"You mean he's been missing for two days?" I said.

"Dad reported it today," said Alan. "The police came over, but I could tell they weren't taking it seriously. They think he's going to turn up in another day or two." He paused. "But I think it *is* serious. Because . . . because of all of this." He gestured around at the miracle we were sharing. "And because you talked to him last night, Henry. I think you were the last person."

"Did you tell the police about that?" said Nicki. "About what Henry saw?"

"No," said Alan. "I didn't know this was real yet. And even if I did . . . I don't know how I would have said it."

"Besides," said Helen, "we can do something *now*, without waiting around for people to decide if we're crazy."

"Henry," said Alan, "what did you mean when you said things were different with Carl?"

And with that single question, we all intuitively decided something, as firmly as if we'd taken a union vote. We were going to look into this ourselves. We'd see if there was anything to it.

"He had flames like ours," I said, "but the snowflakes were all white." I looked up at our own flakes floating around, some soaking into our clothes, others skittering along the ground, or just disappearing up into the night sky. "There are some more," I said, pointing toward my bedroom window, where a bunch of white flakes drifted.

"Why from your room, Henry?" said Helen. "Could it be that guy you saw?"

"What guy?" said Alan.

I filled our friends in on the man who had been (and then not been) in my room. As we looked up at the white flakes in my window, my heart skittered. I didn't really want to meet that man again. But we had to investigate.

We ghosted back through our front door, into the kitchen. Mom and Dad were still at the table, eating their stew. They weren't talking, just seemed lost in thought. It was amazing to see their subtle bodies nested so perfectly inside their regular bodies. Both forms ate at the same time, opening their mouths together and chewing.

But this wasn't what we had come to see.

We continued up the stairs to the second floor.

Just before the entrance to my room, we paused. Everyone looked at me, expecting me to take the lead, but I was too hesitant, and Helen peeked around the corner. "Nobody there," she said. I breathed a sigh of relief, and we entered.

Now that I'd been out for a while and wasn't filling the room with my own flakes, most of the flakes there were white. It was clear where they were coming from.

"The books," said Alan. It was the Airman Crusader series, on my bedside table. Flames licked up from their covers, pouring out pure white flakes. I wondered if *Airman Crusader Versus the Centipede King* had been doing that while I was reading it — blowing gallons of white snowflakes into my face as I read. I wouldn't have been able to see it, in the physical world, but I suppose I was sitting right in the middle of a snowstorm the whole time I was reading. That was more than strange . . . it was downright bizarre.

CHAPTER 8

THE FOLLOWING MORNING at school, the four of us confirmed that we all remembered the same stuff. It wasn't a dream. Incredible as it seemed, we'd walked out of our sleeping bodies and spent the evening together.

In homeroom, McTavish read an announcement—if anyone had any information about Carl Dunn's whereabouts, or about any suspicious persons, they were to contact the police. Furthermore, we should all be careful around town, especially after dark. It was scary to hear that in class. It made everything seem more real.

I thought again about our little group's decision not to tell anyone about the odd things we'd all experienced. I knew of two suspicious people now—the guy who'd been in my room last night and the violinist he'd told me to watch out for. Two characters who very likely had played a role in Carl's disappearance, it seemed to me. But I still thought Helen was right—the four of us could start looking into this right away, rather than waiting for other people to decide if they believed us or not.

When school ended that afternoon, I rushed out of my last class. We'd all arranged to meet at Alan's. I thought Helen and I could get away with it for a few minutes if we went home right after; hopefully Mom and Dad wouldn't notice. I felt awkward about it, and a little guilty. Helen and I hadn't yet told Alan and Nicki that we'd been forbidden to see them. It's hard to tell friends that your parents don't like them.

I hurried to the bike racks to find that Alan's bike was already gone. I unlocked mine, and headed out into another sweltering afternoon.

The Dunns lived in a double-wide trailer that was in pretty poor shape. The flat roof had a lawn growing on it and the gutter on the side leaned away from the downspout. Next to the front door there was a shattered window covered in plastic, and the whole place leaned to one side, like maybe it was about to collapse. If that house had been a horse I'd have shot it out of mercy. The only nice thing about it was the huge front yard. I remembered when Carl had laid out that baseball diamond there, years ago. He'd even installed a pitcher's mound. You'd never know it to look at it now.

The door to the trailer was open, so I stuck my head in. "Alan?" I called. A voice replied: "That Henry Nilsson?" It was Alan's dad, Elmore. "Come in," he rasped.

The front hall to the living room was short but jammed with stuff—a hamper filled with empty beer cans, a chair with a broken seat, a roll of insulating plastic, to name a few things. At the end was the living room, whose only functioning component was an old couch that faced a flickering black and white TV. The sound was down, and a soap opera was on.

Alan's dad was a big man who took up most of the sitting space, a beer on one thigh and his belly on the other. His face was wide and round, his eyes glassy. "What's doing, Henry?" he said. He lifted his beer and gestured with it, inviting me to sit.

I perched uncomfortably on the far edge of the cushion. "Are you waiting for a game to start, Mr. Dunn?" I asked.

"Kind of," he said. His eyes were red. He looked like he might have been crying, but Mr. Dunn often had bloodshot eyes, so I wasn't sure.

"I bet Carl will come home soon," I said.

Mr. Dunn nodded. "You're a nice kid, Henry," he said. "I'm glad you've been friends with my boys."

I didn't bother to correct him that only one of his boys was friends with me, and that the other had recently installed a black eye on my face.

"I'd be out there looking," said Mr. Dunn, "but they said to stay near the phone." He paused. "It's all I can do, anyway," he added. "This damn back of mine." Then he pointed with his beer at the TV screen. "Twins and Rangers," he said. "Alan just stepped to the store for me. He'll be back in a second."

Not sure what to say, I asked, "When did you play for the Twins, sir?" Now that I knew Alan wasn't home, I wanted to go outside and wait, but it seemed rude to leave.

"Fifty-nine," said Mr. Dunn. "Best year of my life." The words sounded strange, without feeling, like the blessing you give before dinner. And the falseness rang out—even Mr. Dunn noticed it. As soon as the words entered the room, he sat up straight, wincing. He looked at the beer on his knee like you'd suddenly seen someone who'd snuck up on you.

Every time I'd chatted with Mr. Dunn (and it wasn't often), he'd been friendly. But something entered his eyes now that I hadn't seen before. Their watery look went icy. His hand tightened around the beer can, crumpling it a little. A seam on the metal broke, and a few drops fell onto the carpet.

I shifted on my seat and looked down into the couch cushions, feeling awkward. And, to my surprise . . . there it was. Jammed between the cushions, I saw a spiral binding and a yellow cover. Carl's notebook.

Mr. Dunn's eyes were on me. "Fifty-nine," he said again, but this time it sounded like a curse. Next to us, the TV screen blanked after a commercial, and a new image appeared: Wrigley Field, from the top of the stands. "They wanted me to fail," Mr. Dunn said, spitting. "Couldn't wait to get rid of me. 'Injun Pitcher Injured,' the headline said."

The sweat I'd poured out on the bike ride went cold. I didn't know what to say, or how to act.

"And now," Mr. Dunn continued, "now my boy's missing, and nobody cares. Just another damn Injun." He leaned forward like he was going to stand up, but he didn't get enough momentum, and he fell back into the couch. He grunted in pain. "I'd be out there right now . . . out there looking for him . . ."

Just then a voice boomed into the hall behind us — a big, deep voice from outside. "Elmore, you there? Any word about Carl?" It was McTavish. I remembered him asking after Carl the day before, and seeming concerned about Alan's home life. And now here he was.

"No word, Ted," Mr. Dunn replied, calming down. "C'mon in." He stood, grimacing, as McTavish entered, wearing a black suit with a white carnation on the lapel.

"You're dressed up," said Mr. Dunn.

"Coming from a funeral," said McTavish.

"Who died?" said Mr. Dunn.

"Did you know Joseph, from Rotary Club?" said McTavish.

Well, McTavish and Mr. Dunn were just jawing away, weren't they? And so . . . I leaned forward, swiped Carl's notebook from between the cushions, and shoved it under my shirt. I swear, I never acted so fast in my life. It seemed like I was watching some other kid.

I stood up nervously, and McTavish turned toward me. "Henry Nilsson," he said, "how's that eye?"

"Getting better, sir," I said.

"I saw your friends outside," he replied. "What are you up to today?"

"Nothing in particular, sir," I said.

"Well, be careful," said McTavish. "We're not certain what's going on here."

"With Carl, you mean?" I said.

"If you see anyone suspicious, Henry," repeated McTavish, "report it to an adult, or the police. You know where the police station is, on Main Street?"

"I know it, sir," I said, holding one hand against my shirt, hoping the notebook didn't show.

"I suppose it's none of my business," said McTavish, "but don't go out after dark, will you, Henry? Promise me that."

"I promise, sir," I said. Half of me, I thought, would keep that promise.

I exited as quickly as I could to the sunny front porch, where Helen and Alan were sitting. Alan had a grocery bag that held a twelve-pack of beer and some corn chips. As I sat with them Nicki pedaled up, rolling to a stop before the three of us.

And with perfect timing (for once), I triumphantly pulled the notebook from under my shirt. "Look at this!" I said.

Alan recognized it instantly. "That's it, Henry! But how—where . . ."

"The couch cushions," I said.

"Open it!" said Helen.

We huddled up and I turned to the first page, which caused us all to gasp. Written across the top line, in a messy hand, were the unmistakable numbers: 1, 1, 2, 3, 5, 8, 13 . . . the exact series we'd all memorized.

"Well, we knew that already," said Nicki. "He must have learned them, or you wouldn't have seen him that first night, Henry."

I flipped a few pages in and we found what we were really after—the notes on Carl's spying. Times, places, things he observed. I saw "Tell Abe" and "Ambulance arrived 5 p.m."

"And here," said Alan, pointing to the bottom. There was the address, just like he'd thought. Fifteen South Half.

"South Half," said Helen. "That must be the Brody mansion."

No sooner had she said it than we all remembered the name: Brody.

"J. Brody," whispered Nicki. "The other author of *Subtle Travel and the Subtle Self*."

"Do you guys know the place?" said Helen.

We all knew it. The Brody mansion was the biggest house around Farro, and the only dwelling along the southern edge of Longbelly Gulch.

"It's almost right across the gulch from Carl's campsite," I said.

Helen and I looked at each other. If we didn't go home now, and at full speed, we could be in pretty bad trouble.

Helen winked at me. I wasn't sure what that meant, entirely, but part of its meaning was that we were in this together, no matter what.

The four of us jumped on our bikes and headed toward the gulch.

CHAPTER 9

AS WE RODE, WE TALKED. It seemed like there was a lot to say . . . or at least a lot to conjecture about.

"So," said Nicki, "we each have two bodies."

"And our heads are on fire," said Alan.

"It's hard to believe," said Helen. "I mean, that our second bodies are right inside us, all the time—even right now! Our heads are on fire right now!" She put both hands on her head, riding for a few moments with no hands (something she was always looking for an excuse to do).

"And Carl knew about it," I said.

"Out in the woods—the book was out there," said Alan. "He learned about it with that guy Abe, I bet."

"You think Abe was teaching him?" said Nicki. "Have you ever seen him? What does he look like?"

"No, I've never seen him," said Alan. "Carl just mentioned him, beginning when summer vacation started. Carl talked about him like . . . well, like he was a coach or something."

"What do you mean?" said Helen.

"He'd say he had to go meet Abe for practice." Alan paused. "And now he's gone. It makes me wonder if, you know, if we might be in some kind of danger here."

"Especially since we're heading straight for the place Carl was spying on," Nicki added.

We reached the turnoff for South Half, and the Brody mansion came into view in the distance, looming by the edge of the gulch. I saw clearly why people called it "mansion" and not "house." It was big, three levels with two separate roof peaks and two chimneys.

The South Half lane, like North Half across the gulch, was oiled dirt, full of bumps and potholes. The woods rose around us and I started feeling a chill, despite the heat of the day. Alan's worries had wormed into me, and all of the unknowns crowded around like watchful crows.

"Alan," I said, hoping to change the subject to a lighter topic, "is Mr. McTavish friends with your dad?"

"Kind of," said Alan. "He's been talking to Dad about getting back to pitching."

"I thought your Dad's back was all messed up," I said.

"McTavish is talking to him about knuckleballs," said Alan.

"Knuckleballs?" I knew the term only vaguely.

"It's a slow pitch," said Alan. "But you can still throw strikes."

"You think your dad could do it?"

"Probably not," said Alan. "But I'm glad someone wants him to try."

We made it to the cement slab in front of the mansion's three-car garage, parked our bikes, and stood together, hesitating. The front door was awfully tall, with a huge brass knocker in the middle.

"We don't know what we're getting into here," I offered, cautiously. "Maybe we should stop and think—"

This immediately set Helen in motion. She strode to the porch, lifted the knocker, and rapped it three times on the striking plate.

Seconds passed.

"Maybe nobody's home," I said.

"Someone's in there," said Nicki. "I hear footsteps."

She was right. Soon we heard a lock unlatch, and the door swung open.

I'd kind of expected to see a butler, like in a movie, but it was an old woman. She was short, partly because she was leaning on a cane. She had shoulder-length gray hair and wore a black dress, black stockings, and black shoes.

Just as I'd expected to see a butler, so she seemed to

have expected someone other than the four of us. She looked angry as she opened the door, but then she became startled.

"I'm Helen Nilsson," Helen announced. "This is my brother, Henry, and our friends Nicki and Alan. We're looking for a man named J. Brody."

The woman opened the door wider. "Perhaps you should come in," she said. She spoke with some kind of accent. It sounded Russian, but there are a hundred accents that sound Russian to me.

Just past the door stretched an enormous living room, full to bursting with an incredible collection of stuff. At the center stood a low coffee table with some fancy photo books on it. Around that, several couches and nice chairs were arranged on a plush red rug. All the walls were hung with possessions—a spear with a stone head next to a mounted trout next to a yellowed world map in a frame. Near that, by the far wall, I saw a big dresser with tiny drawers, like a card catalog, in front of a glass display case filled with jewelry . . . so many interesting things. There was a ship in a bottle. Two woven baskets that were taller than me, a brass sculpture of a deer that was probably heavier than me, and a set of encyclopedias that was probably smarter than me.

While we gawked, the lady hobbled to a chair next to the coffee table and sat, easing herself down with her cane. "Sorry to say, I'm not sure if I've met any of you before. You knew my husband?" she asked.

"Husband?" said Helen.

"Knew?" I said. "Excuse me, Mrs. Brody. But is your husband . . ."

Mrs. Brody nodded. "I assumed that was why you were here," she said. "I've just returned from the funeral. My husband died three days ago — Saturday."

When she said this, I almost cursed out loud, I was so embarrassed. Of course! Joseph Brody — I'd heard Mom mention his death when it was in the paper, and McTavish had been all dressed up from the funeral. I felt terrible. I wanted to curl up and disappear.

"We're very sorry, Mrs. Brody," said Nicki. "We didn't mean to intrude on your grief."

"Oh, yes," said Helen, her cheeks scarlet.

"Very sorry," Alan and I said simultaneously.

"I was about to scold you when I answered the door," said Mrs. Brody. "I asked my friends to give me some time alone. But of course you didn't know." She paused. "Please, sit, and tell me — what did you wish to see my husband about?"

Obediently, we occupied a couch in the order of me, Nicki, Alan, and Helen. My bare knee almost touched Nicki's bare knee. I thought about moving mine across the inch of space, but it might as well have been the distance between the moon and the earth.

"We're looking into a mystery," said Helen. "A missing person."

"My older brother, Carl," said Alan.

"We were hoping Mr. Brody could help us," said Nicki. "We're trying to find out something about a book."

"This book," I said, producing it from my bag and laying it on the coffee table.

Mrs. Brody looked surprised. She bent stiffly forward and took it into her hands. "I've never seen it," she said, "but I know it. My husband wrote it years before we met. And for our whole marriage, he would try to find copies. To buy them, and burn them."

"Burn?" I exclaimed.

"Why did he do that, Mrs. Brody?" said Nicki.

"*Subtle Travel*," said Mrs. Brody, reading the title out loud. "It's so poetic. Where did you find it?"

"In the—" I began, but I sensed Helen bridling next to me. I understood. We should be careful.

Mrs. Brody changed the subject. "It's been a long time since any young people have been in this house," she said.

"Did you raise your children here?" said Nicki.

"My husband and I had no children. We had our work, which I never regretted until now — now that he's gone." She stopped, and I wondered if she was trying not to cry. Old people have a way of just looking old, and sometimes you can't tell what they're feeling. "Please explain more about your missing person," she said.

Given that our most important piece of evidence was my having seen Carl during a midnight out-of-body experience, we didn't leap into explaining.

Mrs. Brody lightly touched the corner of the book with one hand. "You've read it, haven't you? You've used it, and learned the art." She nodded as our faces gave it all away. "You've discovered something in that world. Something that worries you."

"It's true, Mrs. Brody," said Helen. "Only, it sounds crazy."

Mrs. Brody sat quietly, waiting to see if we'd tell the story. When we still hesitated, she said, "Let me go get us all some lemonade."

She stood and walked out of the room, in the direction of the kitchen. The four of us put our heads together and conferred.

"What do you think—should we tell her?" said Helen.

"I vote yes," I said. "I mean, she seems nice enough. And maybe she'll know something. She was married to the guy who wrote the book."

"I agree," said Alan. "Besides, we don't have any other clues."

"I agree, too," said Nicki. "We should learn everything we can."

We separated again hurriedly, but there was no reason to rush. Mrs. Brody was gone for several minutes, and then her voice came from the direction of the kitchen— "Could I get a hand in here?" Helen jumped to service, carrying the lemonade pitcher and glasses, and pouring for everyone. Once Mrs. Brody was seated again, we told her the story. We all participated, me starting out, and then Helen taking it, and then Alan, and then Nicki ending with our arrival on Mrs. Brody's doorstep.

When we finished, Mrs. Brody said, "This man, the one Carl was spying for, is named Abe?"

"Not only spying, either," said Alan. "I think he was, well, a bad influence on Carl."

"I agree," I added, pointing at my own eye.

"Look here, at the cover of the book," said Mrs. Brody, leaning forward and tapping it with a crooked finger. "See the other name—A. Møller. Perhaps you do not know that the A. stands for Abraham. Your evidence suggests that my husband's one-time collaborator has returned to Iowa."

"You know him?" I said, amazed.

"I know of him," said Mrs. Brody. "Oh, I wish Joseph were still alive," she said, and then added, "Forgive my tears," though there were no tears on her face.

It was weird to think that Mr. and Mrs. Brody had probably been married for twice as long as I'd been alive. I couldn't imagine what that would be like. Helen, of course, always had something to contribute. "When our grandpa died last year," she said, "Grandma died three months later." I winced inwardly.

"I'm not quite ready for that," said Mrs. Brody, a note of amusement in her voice.

"Tell us more about Abe Møller," said Helen, forging ahead. "What do you know about him?"

"He was the reason my husband wished to destroy the books," said Mrs. Brody. "I should add that Joseph hated almost no one in this world. He was a very loving person. But he hated Abraham Møller." She turned to Alan. "And so I think your brother, if he is meeting with this man, is surely in danger." She took up the book again and flipped through a few pages. Something seemed to catch her eye. "Well, what do you know," she said. "Fibonacci."

"What's that?" said Helen.

"Have you recited these numbers — 1, 1, 2, 3, 5, and the rest?"

"Yes, it's an important part," I said.

"But you don't know what they are?" said Mrs. Brody. None of us did.

"This is the Fibonacci sequence. Joseph was always interested in it. See here." She picked up a pencil and a bit of scratch paper from the table. In a shaky hand, she wrote out the numbers, ending with 21 and 34, and then added 55, 89, and 144.

"How are you doing that?" said Nicki.

"A good puzzle," said Mrs. Brody. "I should leave you with it."

"Tell us!" Helen shouted, spilling a little of her lemonade. Mrs. Brody laughed.

"The final two integers are the addends for the next,"

she explained. She wrote 89 + 144 = 233, then 144 + 233 = 377.

"But . . . why do we have to say them?" I said. "I mean, what do they do?"

"It's part of the world," said Mrs. Brody. "You see it in nature — the way petals are arranged on a rose, or branchlets on a tree." She paused. "It's not surprising to me that such a pattern could lead the mind onward, like a plant growing."

"But brains aren't plants," I said.

"Aren't they?" said Mrs. Brody. "My husband once told me that this sequence was first discovered in India, and was used as a technique in poetry. So you see, not so far removed — the growth of a bud into a bloom, and the growth of a mind into a poem. Two kinds of opening up. And that is precisely the art you are studying, is it not? To open the mind?"

"Wow," said Nicki. "We could definitely use your help, Mrs. Brody."

I think we all confronted, at that moment, that we were just a bunch of kids and that Mrs. Brody might know all kinds of important things. Even so, we were a little taken aback at what she said next.

"Would you lend me this book?" she asked. "If I could join you in this . . . this subtle world, I might be more useful."

We exchanged quick glances among ourselves. My glance said, *We need to think about this.*

"Um, could we talk that over really fast, Mrs. Brody? With just us?" said Helen.

"Of course," said Mrs. Brody. Slowly, she picked up the empty lemonade pitcher and made her way out to the kitchen.

Once again, we put our heads together.

"What do you guys think?" said Helen.

"She seems nice," I said. "And smart."

"She knew those numbers," said Alan. "I think she could help us."

"But what if we get her into trouble?" said Nicki. "What if this ends up being dangerous? She's pretty old."

"That's a good point," I said. "I wouldn't want to drag her in if it's risky."

"She's an adult," said Helen. "She can get into trouble if she wants."

That seemed to decide it. Helen stood and headed toward the kitchen. The rest of us followed, bringing our empty glasses.

The kitchen was much larger than any I'd seen, with a huge bank of windows along one side looking into Longbelly Gulch and the forest. It was beautiful, with light streaming in everywhere.

Mrs. Brody was just putting the empty pitcher into the sink as Helen announced, "You can borrow the book."

"But on one condition," I added.

"Condition?" said Helen, turning toward me.

"What is your condition, Henry?" said Mrs. Brody.

"That we stay the night here," I said, "to make sure you're safe. And that you call our mom to tell her we're helping you with . . . with some housework."

"Henry! That is genius!" Helen exclaimed. I had to admit, it was pretty good. Mom had just been saying she felt sad about Mrs. Brody. Now we were helping her. Surely our parents couldn't get angry about that, even if we'd disobeyed our grounding.

"Well, I'm very touched," said Mrs. Brody. "Of course you can stay. That is, if you aren't afraid . . ."

"Afraid?" said Helen. Fear for her was like a TV show she was looking forward to.

Mrs. Brody pointed to the near wall, at a framed picture there. "A photo of myself and my husband, taken many years ago," she said. "You'll find quite a few through the house. Have a look at it."

The picture was black and white. It showed Mr. and Mrs. Brody standing with their arms around each other, gazing into each other's eyes. They looked about the age of our parents. Even so, you could recognize Mrs. Brody's little chin. Mr. Brody was a tall man with narrow shoulders. His hair was black. He had twinkling eyes, and one of those mustaches where the ends tip upward like a smile.

"You see how much we loved each other," said Mrs. Brody.

"What's he holding there?" said Nicki. "Is it a violin case?"

Violin! The word jumped out at me, taking me right back to my bedroom and the mysterious man who had questioned me. I looked closely at the picture. Was Mr. Brody the violinist I'd been warned about? If so, then the mysterious man was looking for someone he'd never find. Still it sent a chill up my spine.

"He was a wonderful performer, from a family of musicians," said Mrs. Brody. "He wooed me with that violin, and we buried him with it today. I thought, if he has it, maybe he'll play for me when I cross over one day."

"How did your husband die?" said Helen.

"He'd been unwell for some time," said Mrs. Brody. "Heart troubles. He passed away upstairs, in our bedroom, just before the ambulance arrived." She paused. "Now this house is too big, too empty. Which brings me back to the thing that might scare you."

"Yes, what is it?" said Helen.

"Maybe it's just me, but I've thought a few times in the past days that Joseph's ghost is here somewhere."

"The ghost of your husband?" I said, and just then, out of nowhere, a big orange house cat jumped up onto the kitchen counter right in front of me. I let out an embarrassing yelp.

"Hello, Oscar," said Mrs. Brody. She nudged the cat's wide head with one hand, and he nudged her back, then looked away, out into the living room. "I think he sees the ghost," she said.

CHAPTER 10

MOM THOUGHT IT WAS a great idea for us to stay over-night to help Mrs. Brody around her house. She wanted to be mad, but you can't be mad when your kids are coming to the aid of an old, widowed woman. "Genius," said Helen again as I worked this out on the phone.

Nicki got permission from her parents, too. I wasn't sure which way it would go, since it was a school night—but she explained that she usually got what she wanted because she so rarely asked for anything. ("Interesting strategy," Helen mused.)

Alan's permission took about two seconds—he just told his dad where he was. I heard a baseball game in the background. I was a little surprised that Mr. Dunn wasn't more worried, given the situation with Carl. But I dimly heard his voice slurring on the phone, and thought maybe he didn't exactly know what he was agreeing to.

So, the four of us returned to our houses to get our

overnight things, and then met up to bike again along the south edge of the gulch as afternoon turned into evening.

"I just remembered something, you guys," I said as we traversed the bumpy way. "That night, when I saw Carl—he was talking about a ghost. Just like Mrs. Brody was."

"Do you think he meant someone's subtle form?" said Nicki.

"We were already in our subtle forms," I said. "I think he really meant a ghost."

We coasted onto the cement slab outside the three-car garage, parked our bikes, and knocked on the front door. Now I understood why we had to wait so long—Mrs. Brody, using her cane, walking slowly through the huge place. This time it was almost five minutes before the lock turned.

"Hello again," said Mrs. Brody, smiling.

After we dropped off our overnight bags in the living room, Mrs. Brody went to a side door, made of sliding glass. "I'm hoping you'll help me cross the gulch, my friends, before we have dinner. I'd like to visit Joseph's grave again before nightfall."

This struck me as a good thing to do. I wanted to pay my respects. Still, knowing that Mr. Brody's ghost might be floating around nearby was a little unsettling.

Mrs. Brody gathered a few cut flowers from a vase, and we exited the house onto a narrow dirt path that zigzagged down the gulch to Longbelly Creek. If I were to have run the distance, I'd have been at the bottom in two minutes. With Mrs. Brody, it took almost fifteen.

A flat bridge, somewhat dilapidated, spanned the narrow creek, ending where the trail resumed up the north slope.

"Joseph and I built it when we moved here," said Mrs. Brody.

We crossed, and followed the trail up the switchbacks to North Half, then walked to a turnoff, where we saw an old wooden sign that said "Graveyard," before an iron fence. I opened the gate, which creaked as graveyard gates do. Then I heard another sound. I put a hand to my ear, listening.

"What is it, Henry?" said Alan.

"Those branches," I said. "Remember the branches we heard at the campsite? I bet it's the same ones. That's how close we are."

"Wow, weird," said Helen. "It seemed like we were in

the middle of nowhere, but we were barely behind this place."

"What are you all discussing?" asked Mrs. Brody.

"My brother," said Alan. "He had a campsite in the woods just behind here."

The graveyard was not particularly kept up. The grass was brown and long. The plots near the road were spaced closely, but dispersed the farther we went, and there was no clear end to the place. It just petered out into the forest.

We found an area where the long grass was all trampled, and then reached the new grave, with raw dirt around the edges, and piled on top of it a mound of flowers. I'd never seen so many, and all kinds—carnations, and roses . . . I don't know many flower names. At the top of the grave stood a dark gray headstone of polished marble, set perfectly straight, like the headboard of a bed. It immediately reminded me of how people say death is like sleep.

The gravestone was inscribed: "Joseph A. Brody, 1890–1963, Beloved Husband & Author." Mrs. Brody, using her cane, knelt and placed the flowers she'd brought, right where the pillow would go if the grave really was a bed.

"Did your husband write other books besides *Subtle Travel?*" I asked.

"He and I wrote many books together," said Mrs. Brody. "A series. I'll show you back at the house."

She put one old hand on the curved top of the gravestone, and spoke to her husband. "Joseph," she said, "do you see these nice young people? They helped me cross the creek. I may not be able to come every day, Joseph, because of my knees, but I'll come as often as I can."

"I wish we could have met him," said Helen.

"You'd have liked him," said Mrs. Brody. She smiled sadly. "Maybe you'll meet his ghost."

CHAPTER 11

WHEN THE NOODLES CAME OUT of the boiling water, Mrs. Brody sent Helen and me into the dining room with the silverware while Nicki and Alan helped plate the food. Oscar the cat was sitting on the table, and I shooed him off. Helen and I set five places.

Mrs. Brody sat at the head, and before we dug in she held up her hands, as high as her stooped shoulders, and recited a blessing. It was not in English, and it also did not sound much like Russian. When she finished I asked, "What language was that, Mrs. Brody?"

"Call me Maria," she said. "That prayer is in Hebrew, the language of the Jews, of whom I am one."

I hadn't known Mrs. Brody was Jewish. In fact, she was the first Jewish person I had ever met, I think. "Did you write books in Hebrew?" I asked.

"Oh, I promised I would show you," said Mrs. Brody. She stood, went to a bookshelf on a near wall, and pulled down a volume, which she brought to the table and placed between me and Helen. On the cover was a picture of a snow-capped mountain. The title was *International Understanding Travel Guides — China.* "Joseph and I started writing these after the war," said Mrs. Brody.

I opened the book and saw that it was not written in Hebrew, but English.

"I came to the U.S. in 1939," Mrs. Brody continued as she returned to her seat. "I escaped the worst of Europe, and watched the war from here."

"World War . . . Two?" I said, a little embarrassed at how poor my history was.

"I'm from Poland," said Mrs. Brody. "My family — my parents and my brother and his family — we fled the Nazis to Lithuania. We left in the middle of the night, at the moment of the September Campaign." Mrs. Brody paused. "Travel books were a long ways off, then. We were refugees. From Lithuania to Sweden, and finally to here. Iowa. Isn't it odd? In Iowa I found love. Joseph and I married after armistice. We shared a belief, he and I, that there should be no more war. People must strive to understand one another, especially in this atomic age. That's why we chose the title for our books: *International Under-*

standing. And the message was popular. The books were successful."

I passed the book to Helen. She flipped through, looking at the black-and-white pictures of various locations and sites in China. "I've never been anywhere," she said, "but I want to go everywhere."

"And the rest of you?" said Mrs. Brody. "Will you travel?"

"I haven't thought about it," said Alan. "My dad went places when he was in the majors, but he says he only saw airports and ball fields."

"I'd like to go to China," said Nicki, taking the book from Helen. "See where my great-grandparents came from."

"And you, Henry?" said Mrs. Brody.

"Our dad traveled a little," I said. "He went to Korea for a year."

"As a soldier," Mrs. Brody guessed. "But tell me if you want to travel, Henry — and where you'd go."

"To outer space," said Helen, elbowing me. "Henry wants to be an astronaut."

"Oh, yeah," I said. "She's right."

"Into the emptiness," said Mrs. Brody.

"But not empty," I said. "There could be aliens out there."

"So, you are a reader of science fiction stories, then?" said Mrs. Brody.

"Yes . . ." I said, and, remembering, I went to my book-bag in the living room, and brought back my copy of *Airman Crusader*. I handed it to Mrs. Brody.

She recognized the author's name. "I've heard of these," she said. "Joseph mentioned them. He said Abe Møller earned an easy living by them." She flipped to the first page, and then the next, and then the next. She was a fast reader. "Such books as this," she said, "are not really about outer space, Henry. Have you learned that?"

"Um . . . er . . ." I said, because I was pretty sure that they were about outer space.

"They are about us. About people. They are about me, Henry—the alien."

I stared back, not sure how to understand what she'd just said. Alien?

"This is always the question I have about science fiction stories," Mrs. Brody continued. "How do they treat the alien? You see, Henry, the United States calls me a 'resident alien.' I'm an alien being from another country.

Books such as this one have heroes that dislike my kind. They go to my home, they exterminate me. This reveals something about our friend Abe Møller, this attitude. He prefers extermination to understanding. Contempt to sympathy."

"That happened to my people, too," said Alan, suddenly. "I mean, I don't really know if they're my people, I guess, but I'm part Nez Perce. My dad's three-quarters. And when you say that, it just reminds me. In school we learn about how Christopher Columbus discovered America and stuff . . . but my dad says Columbus was an invader who came here to kill Indians."

I'd never heard Mr. Dunn, or anyone, say anything like that. It was a mighty strange way to think about the Pilgrims. But it kind of made sense. "The centipedes in the book were like people," I said. "They lived in cities." I shook my head. I hadn't ever thought about science fiction this way.

"These are complex ideas," Mrs. Brody replied. "I can only tell you my belief that sympathy will never do harm. But contempt—contempt is the trap. It holds the mind like iron, and leads men to brutality. When someone is considered less than human, when they are a . . . a centipede," Mrs. Brody said, pointing to the cover of the book, "you don't have to treat them kindly. You can misuse them in the service of getting what you want."

"Airman Crusader wanted to live forever," I said. "In this book, he's trying to find a potion for immortality. He thought the centipede creatures had it."

"There's nothing wrong with wanting to live," said Mrs. Brody, "except when you make others suffer for it."

"Something doesn't make sense about what you said before, Mrs. Brody," said Helen. "About being sympathetic. You said your husband hated Abe Møller. That wasn't very sympathetic of him."

Mrs. Brody nodded. "Joseph told me he did try, for a time, to understand Abraham, but he failed. He told me it was like with certain men during the war. You see, men who had been *made* cruel were the common type, then. Twisted from their better natures by circumstance. But for a few, cruelty seemed natural. They are one in ten thousand, such people, and you are correct, Helen, that it is a very serious accusation to make against someone. You can never be absolutely sure. We cannot see souls with our earthly eyes."

After dinner, we went to the living room and Mrs. Brody showed us some of her antiques. She removed two pieces of silver jewelry from a display case—a necklace and a bracelet. "Family heirlooms," she said, handing one to Helen and the other to Nicki. "The necklace belonged to my great-grandmother. The bracelet was her sister's."

"What country did you say you were you from?" I asked.

"Poland," said Mrs. Brody. "My family lived there for generations. Not now, of course."

"Everyone left, during the war?" I asked.

"Not left, Henry," she said. "They were murdered." She paused. "I returned once, years after the war, to see the graveyard where my parents and grandparents were buried. It is all weeds now. There are no Jews left to care for their own dead." Then she said, "These are reasons people must travel. And not as your father did, Henry— not to make war. But to learn. To welcome the alien into your heart."

CHAPTER 12

WE DECIDED TO SLEEP in the living room, on the couches. Mrs. Brody told us where she kept the extra blankets—upstairs in the closet at the end of the hall—and Nicki and I went to get them.

It was kind of dark up there, without many windows, but we stopped to look at a few of the old photos hung along the way, mostly of Mrs. and Mr. Brody.

It's so funny to have a crush on someone. I was thrilled to be alone with Nicki. My heart was beating a million times a second . . . and yet it was awful too. I worried that everything I did or said would be wrong. My mind veered. I tried to think of good jokes, or intelligent observations, but it all got gummed up, and suddenly I found myself saying something that was neither funny nor smart. I said, "Nicki, my parents have grounded us from seeing you and Alan."

Nicki turned toward me. "What, Henry? But . . . why?"

"I don't know," I said. "They really let us have it after

the fight with Carl. They kind of went crazy." I paused. "I think maybe your dad got a job my dad was applying for."

"He just started this week," she replied, "with Bell Telephone."

"My dad wanted it," I said. "And he said he had more experience than your dad. He said . . . something about civil rights, and immigrants."

Nicki nodded, her eyes growing intense. "He thinks my dad got the job because he's Chinese," she said. "Is that right?"

"Gosh, I feel terrible," I said. "I'm sorry I didn't say anything before . . ."

"It isn't your fault, Henry," she said. "I'm sorry your dad hasn't found work. I hope he does. But he's wrong about my dad. Nobody ever gave him anything he didn't deserve." Nicki paused, and I could tell she was going to continue, so I waited. "All the names around here," she said. "Andersson. Johansson. Nilsson. My dad joked that we should change our name to Chensson, so maybe we'd fit in better."

I wasn't sure how to respond to this. Chensson would be a very odd name. It was obviously a joke, but Nicki wasn't laughing.

"You know how my family got to Iowa, Henry?" she asked.

"You mean, from China?" I said.

"It was the railroad. My great-grandfather worked on the Transcontinental Railroad. And in Iowa he got attacked by an Irish railroad gang. They mobbed him and some other Chinese workers, saying that Chinese people were stealing Irish jobs. They almost killed him, and he ended up in the hospital in Cedar Rapids. He was stranded here."

I'd never heard this before. I didn't know if Helen even knew this story.

"*Apparently* Chinese people steal jobs from white people all the time," Nicki said bitterly. "Maybe it's our strongest racial trait. So it makes sense that my dad stole your dad's new job." She paused, breathing kind of hard. "Henry, did you know I applied to the Advanced Humanities program at school this year?"

"Helen told me you got in," I said.

"I did," said Nicki. "But some parents complained. Some parents, I don't know who, said I cheated. And the school made me retake the exam." She clenched her hands into fists. "They accused me . . . of stealing someone's place."

"Gosh, Nicki," I said. "I'm so sorry . . . I never thought . . ."

"Why should you?" she snapped. Then she sighed. "I'm sorry, Henry. It just tires me out."

We reached the cabinet at the end of the hall, where Mrs. Brody had said the blankets would be. I opened it. "Nicki," I said, "I . . . I really like you. I mean, if there's anything . . . if you ever need anyone to talk to . . ."

"I like you too, Henry," said Nicki as I reached in and removed an armful of blankets. I turned to hand them to her.

And I found, to my surprise, that she was staring right at me. Inches from me. I froze, and my whole body filled with a weird electricity that was half terror and half astonishment. I knew if the moment lasted longer, I'd do something. I wasn't sure what. She was so beautiful . . .

Awkwardly, I shoved the blankets into her arms and turned away to get more, exclaiming, "These are really good blankets," which is the stupidest thing anyone has ever said.

I grabbed another armful and we headed back down the hall. My knees were shaking. I cursed myself for being such a coward. I should have asked her. I should have said, Will You Go To the Fall Formal With Me? Probably twenty guys were calling her house right now.

Back in the living room, the four of us made up four couches with the blankets. We took turns brushing our teeth in the downstairs bath and changing into pajamas, and soon we were sitting on our makeshift beds. Mrs. Brody stood at the foot of the stairs, preparing to head up to her room. "When I awake in my subtle form tonight," she said, "I'll come out and meet all of you." She smiled.

"You'll be wearing whatever you wear to bed," said Helen.

"Good to know," said Mrs. Brody. She ascended the stairs slowly with the help of her cane, like a mountain climber, and then the four of us were alone in the huge living room.

"Helen," said Nicki, "Henry told me about what happened. With you being grounded."

"Grounded?" said Alan.

We explained to him too, and we all agreed that my parents were crazy. We'd just keep looking for ways to disobey without them finding out. Then Alan turned off the large lamp in the corner of the living room and Helen turned off the small one on the coffee table. The room went dark except for the pale light of the moon shining through the windows.

I pulled my blanket up to my ears. On the couch next to me, Nicki snuggled under her own blanket. We all propped our arms up. We began to count.

CHAPTER 13

I HEARD ELVIS. His voice was high and fragile, and I thought he was singing "Are You Lonesome Tonight?" But then the voice went higher, and lasted longer, and stretched out, and became strange.

I opened my eyes.

Above me, the starry sky.

I sat up. All around in the darkness were dim gravestones, set in rows like hospital beds. The shadows of the trees cast by the moon lay over everything. The sound I'd thought was Elvis continued — two branches creaking together, far back in the forest.

I was in Longbelly Cemetery.

Terrified, I lurched to my feet and tried to run, but something was holding on to my ankle. I fell hard and scrambled on all fours like a trapped raccoon, swatting, twisting.

I looked back at my leg and saw the mouth of a huge animal, exposed white teeth sinking into my calf over my jeans. But it wasn't an animal—it was teeth only, attached to a length of chain set in a hook in the ground. It was a trap, similar to a bear trap, but bright white instead of black iron, like compacted snow.

I think if I could have left my leg behind at that moment, I would have. My guts churning, I grabbed the chain with both hands and rattled it against the loop in the ground. I dimly registered that this was the first time I'd successfully held something with my subtle hands, but I was too panicked to appreciate it. The only thought in my head was escape. I swear, I'd never been so scared.

My subtle eyes could see well in the darkness. About twenty feet off was Mr. Brody's grave with its new stone, covered in flowers. Then I saw something else, which made me forget all of that. I saw fire—a bright flickering, and rainbow snowflakes emerging from the head of a man who sat about fifteen feet away. He was leaning against a nearby gravestone, his hands on his bent knees, kind of slouching as if he'd been there for a while. He was looking right at me.

With great effort, I calmed my racing heart. I could barely breathe, but I spoke. "Who are you?" I said, my voice loud in the darkness. "What do you want?"

I awakened.

I was under my blanket, back at Mrs. Brody's. The lights were turned on, and at the top of the stairs stood Mrs. Brody, wearing a flannel nightgown. "I saw him!" she called down to us, excitedly. "I saw him true!"

"Who?" said Alan, sitting up.

"My husband," said Mrs. Brody. "It was Joseph."

"Here, in the house?" said Helen.

"No, outside. Through the window I saw him. In the woods. He was wearing the suit we buried him in. He had his violin case."

"What was he doing?" said Helen.

"Walking," she said, "toward the gulch."

"Henry, where were you?" said Helen. "You never appeared."

Shakily, I told my story. Mrs. Brody joined us as I described what had happened. "I think I'm still out there," I said. "I'm out there, and I'm trapped."

CHAPTER 14

OF COURSE, SCHOOL WASN'T canceled just because my subtle body was stuck in a graveyard bear trap. My friends and I still had to get up as usual. Mrs. Brody made us oatmeal with maple syrup. Before we left, she asked if I'd like to borrow one of the travel books she wrote with her husband. I picked *International Understanding Travel Guides — China*, remembering that was the country Nicki said she'd like to visit.

Then we rode through the cool morning air toward school, the road steaming as the early sun struck it. Now that it was daytime the dark graveyard seemed distant, and I hoped that what happened had been some kind of fluke — that I wouldn't find myself there again tonight.

"Henry," said Nicki, pedaling alongside me. "Do you think you're still out there, chained up? Can you tell?"

"We've got to rescue you, Henry," said Alan.

"Tonight," said Helen. "We'll pry that trap off and clobber that guy!"

Suddenly I put on the brakes. I rolled to a stop, and everyone else stopped too. "No," I said, firmly. "We need to think this through. You guys could get caught just like me. If I'm still out there tonight, I'm going to try to talk to him, whoever he is." This idea scared me, but it seemed right. Also, I wanted to be brave and sensible in front of Nicki. I glanced at her, but I couldn't tell if she was impressed. She just looked worried.

After a little more insisting on my part, my friends agreed to wait a night before rescuing me. "I just don't like it, Henry," said Helen. "You always want to think about stuff. What's to think about? You're in trouble!" But she could see that I had a good point. Truthfully, it was kind of funny to me, Helen having to wait. Waiting to rescue me, and waiting for Alan to ask her to the dance . . . she looked like she was about to pop.

We reached homeroom and all sat together as the bell rang and Mr. McTavish entered. Watching him come through the door, with his giant shoulders, was kind of like watching someone maneuver a sofa, I thought . . . and then my heart clenched in my chest.

I stood up.

I rushed past the tables, through the door, and out into the hall.

"Henry!" Helen shouted, following instantly, clueing in to my panic with a twinsy quickness. "What's wrong?"

My feet had developed a mind of their own. I zoomed outside and toward the bike racks, where Helen caught me by the arm and dragged me to a stop.

"It's McTavish," I said, breathing hard. "It's him. He's the one in the graveyard with me."

Needless to say, I waited out the remainder of homeroom there at the bike racks with my sister.

CHAPTER 15

MOM AND DAD WERE HOME when we got back from school—the car was out front. Helen and I parked our bikes and went into the kitchen. Mom was there, at the table, in her work dress. Dad too, wearing his gray jumpsuit. The car keys were in his hand, so I knew they were about to go. I could tell with a glance that they were both in a bad mood.

Mom stood immediately and said, "We're just leaving, you two. You'll have to cook again tonight."

"That's fine," I said. "I'll make corn chowder."

Dad took a deep breath and let it out as he got up, something he only did when he was trying to calm himself. I glanced at Helen to see if she was picking up on this. For once, she didn't do anything to make it worse.

"How did things go with Mrs. Brody last night?" Mom asked.

"I think she's okay," I said. "We helped out in the

kitchen." I turned to my sister. "Let's get started on dinner, Helen."

"We'll see you both tomorrow," said Mom. She and Dad exited, and the screen door slapped shut behind them.

When they were safely gone, I said, "That was close."

"What was he so mad about?" said Helen.

"I don't know," I said. I went to the refrigerator and got out a plastic bag full of corn ears, then took the soup pot from the lowest drawer and sat at the table. "Grab a couple knives, will you?" I said. "I want to get this on the stove before *The Dead of Night* starts."

"That's not till later," said Helen.

"There's an afternoon rerun," I said. "You know I always watch it."

"Henry, I've been thinking," said Helen. She took two knives from the block and handed me one as she sat. I started stripping cobs and throwing kernels into the soup pot as she continued. "Why did Mr. McTavish trap you out there, in the graveyard? It has to have something to do with Carl, right?"

"I don't know," I said. "It's so strange—McTavish always seemed like a pretty good guy. Alan said he's been trying to get his dad to start pitching again."

"It just doesn't add up," said Helen. "Carl didn't mention McTavish when you saw him—you know, that first night you used the book?"

"No," I said. "Nothing with Carl connects to McTavish. Carl's connected to the Brodys, spying on them, because Abe Møller told him to—"

"But why is Møller here, in Farro? Why was he using Carl to spy on the Brodys? They weren't doing anything."

"But they did do something," I said. "I mean, kind of. Mr. Brody died."

"Hmm," said Helen. "That's interesting. Maybe that's what Møller wanted to know—that Mr. Brody was dead. And now you're trapped out in the graveyard where Brody's buried. Didn't you say you could see the grave from where you are?"

"Yeah, I'm maybe twenty feet from it. The trap was set right there."

"Weird we didn't see it when we went out with Mrs. Brody."

"I think it only exists in the subtle world," I said. "We would have seen it for sure. It's bright white. It covers my whole shoe. It's like . . . a subtle trap."

Helen stopped working when I said that, and gave

me a quizzical glance. "Did you wear shoes to bed?" she asked.

"No, I didn't," I said. "Yeah, that's weird. Shouldn't I be wearing my pajamas? But I'm not—I'm wearing the clothes I had on earlier."

"Henry," said Helen, "I think you walked into that trap while we were out there, visiting the grave!"

"Gosh, you're right! It snared me, and I . . . just walked away from myself."

"We've got to save you, Henry," she said. "We've got to go out there."

"Not yet," I said. "Now that I know it's McTavish, I want to try to talk to him."

Helen was not enthusiastic about this idea. "Yeah, just ask him, 'What is your nefarious plan, sir?' I'm sure he'll explain."

"Where did you learn the word *nefarious*?" I said.

"You aren't the only one who knows words, Henry. Now listen, here's what we should do—we should spy on him. Like, sneak into his house." Helen's eyes lit up in a way I did not like as she said this.

"No way," I said. "Let's finish these and watch TV."

We stripped the last few ears of corn and I combined

the rest of the ingredients to make the soup. Then I put it on the range to heat up and we headed into the living room.

We stepped through the doorway, and stopped.

Right there, where our TV should have been, there was nothing. The carpet was pressed down into a neat, empty rectangle.

The pieces fell into place. All of the belt-tightening, the shift cuts, the rail strike . . .

"He pawned it," I said, a little awestruck.

Helen waved her hand in the space, feeling the air there. Then we both sat on the couch.

"Now I understand why he was so angry he didn't get that job," I said.

Our eyes fell on the coffee table, where Dad had left the evening paper. The headline said, "Nationwide Rail Strike Set for Midnight." Next to that was another head-line: "D.C. Prepares for Violence." It was an article about the big civil rights march that was going to happen to-morrow.

The two of us sat silently. We were both confused. Strikes, marches . . . it was all too big. I couldn't get my mind around it.

"I know where he lives," said Helen, abruptly.

"Who?" I said.

"Mr. McTavish. He's up the street from the Dunns. One of those new houses on Anderssen Street."

"Oh, we shouldn't—" I said.

"We gotta, Henry."

"Helen, think—"

"No more thinking!" said Helen. She jumped to her feet.

"But we really need to think—"

"Henry, you're like a broken record!" said Helen, and she zoomed out of the house, to her bike.

Well, there was no TV to watch.

I put the soup on simmer, and followed.

A couple streets over from Alan's, on a block of new one-level homes, we hid our bikes in the bushes and hiked behind the houses. Each one had a back porch and screen door.

"This blue one," said Helen, pointing. "This is him."

"We should stop and think—" I began.

"Shush," said Helen, "you'll get us caught." As if any trouble here was my fault. "He's not home," she said, scanning the street. "See his driveway? You know his car."

McTavish drove a red Chevy, and Helen was right— it wasn't there.

"He's probably at practice," I said.

We walked onto the back lawn and up to the porch. Helen climbed the steps like they were her own, turned the knob on the door, opened it . . . and then, for the first time in my life, I was trespassing in someone's house.

I was scared, thinking we'd find McTavish standing right there. Maybe his car was at the shop, or maybe someone was borrowing it, or maybe he'd sold it . . . why had I not thought of any of this a minute ago? But as we stood in the silent living room, it became apparent that the house was empty.

"I guess there's a first time for everything," I whispered.

"First time?" said Helen.

"Breaking into someone's house," I said.

"First time for you maybe," said Helen.

"You've done this before?"

"Not here," said Helen as she strode confidently forward, "but other places."

"Helen, why?" I said. "It's not right."

"It's interesting," said Helen. "You get to see how peo-ple live. Did you know that the Murgutroys have —"

"Shush!" I said. "Don't tell me."

Helen snickered. "Okay, Mr. Proper, now help me find some clues."

McTavish's living room was a lot like ours. I hadn't ex-pected that from someone I now thought of as a supernat-ural kidnapper, but here was a pretty nice couch that was a similar color to ours, sitting in front of a TV that was the same brand we used to have. I found myself staring at the screen a little jealously.

"Henry, get cracking!" said Helen.

"Sorry," I said, "it's just that *The Dead of Night* is on right now."

We started searching. It's funny, I've read some detec-tive stories where people break into places looking for clues. They always go to a back room and open a filing cabinet, and then say, "Here it is!" But where is that back room? McTavish did not appear to own a filing cabinet. While Helen breezed through the kitchen and disap-peared down a hall, I examined the living room.

There were a few framed photos sitting on a corner ta-ble. One showed McTavish with his arm around a brown-haired woman. She was really big, kind of like him, but they didn't look similar otherwise. I squinted at the photo. As far as I knew, McTavish wasn't married.

I went into the kitchen, even though Helen had already been through it, and saw a calendar with notes in some of the squares, like "Rotary Club" or "Haircut" or "Baseball." I saw Mr. Brody's funeral written in for this past Tuesday, the date circled in red. There was one other date circled in red—tomorrow. But there was nothing written. That seemed kind of ominous.

I was ready to go, but Helen was still rooting around elsewhere, and I knew if I asked her to hurry she'd do the opposite. She'd hide in a closet and stay all night, even.

So I returned to the living room to wait. I stared forward into the blank eye of the TV. Well, I thought, as long as I'm here anyway . . .

I turned it on. The little dot appeared, and the tube whined as it warmed up. I sat on the couch. The dot brightened, and burst into the world of my favorite show. What was more, even though it was a rerun, it was an episode I'd never seen before. I was captivated. A rich old man sat in his enormous living room, which was way nicer even than Mrs. Brody's. He was sipping wine, and around him were a bunch of clocks, all ticking. Then the clocks stopped and the Devil appeared—tall, with a black cloak and the horns and tail. "You've grown old," said the Devil, laughing. "Soon you'll die, and you'll lose all of these riches. But what if you could live forever? What would you do . . . for all the time in the world?"

"Forever . . . ?" said the old man. At that moment, all of his clocks started ticking again. They'd been ticking his life away for years, and I could tell that the idea of Forever was the most beautiful thing in the world to this old man. He looked around at all of his possessions. "I would do anything," he said.

Just then Helen, a little deflated, entered and sat next to me. "Okay," she said, "I struck out. Let's go."

"No," I said, not even turning to look at her.

She saw my gaze trained on the TV. "Oh, okay," she said. She normally wasn't very interested in *The Dead of Night*, but this episode seemed to grab her attention.

The Devil told the rich man he'd live forever if he could find two people to take his place. In other words, if he murdered two people, the Devil would grant him immortality.

The rich man agreed, and went out looking for victims. In a dingy, small park he found two bums drunk on a bench. Clearly, they didn't deserve to live as much as he did. He went home and mixed some rat poison into a bottle of whiskey, intending to give it to the hoboes. Then the show took a commercial break. I'd seen the first ad a ton of times, for a fancy kind of vacuum. It started with a husband coming home from work, opening the front door.

Only, the sound of the door didn't come from the screen.

It came from behind us.

Helen and I both whipped around on the couch, and saw McTavish standing there.

I gulped a breath of air, which I thought might be my last as McTavish's little eyes bored into us from behind his horn-rimmed glasses. His huge black beard looked like the smoke of hellfire. In one arm, he held a brown grocery bag.

He didn't speak, just looked at us. He closed the door behind him and walked into the kitchen, out of sight. I heard him put the grocery bag down, and I turned to Helen to see if she wanted to make a break for it—but McTavish returned too soon. He crossed the room, each footfall so heavy I could feel it reverberate through the floor. He sat across from us, next to the TV in a cane chair, and turned down the volume knob as the episode came back on—but I wasn't paying attention anymore. I was staring at McTavish, sweating bullets.

Really, I should be in tears right now, I thought, and was surprised that I wasn't. Yet I heard some of the sounds I usually make when I cry. The quick intakes of breath, and the nervous wheezing.

I turned to Helen and saw something I'd never witnessed before: the failure of her courage. If the situation hadn't been so serious, it would have been funny, because she barely knew how to cry. Her shoulders went up and down like pistons, and a little chirp came out each time.

Soon she quieted enough to take a panicked gulp of air and say, as a warning, I guess, "Our dad is a soldier. He's—he's killed people."

McTavish nodded. "Hopefully it won't come to that," he said. "But you are trespassing in my home. I think I deserve an explanation."

Strange. Here we were, alone with the guy who'd kidnapped my subtle form, and he was putting on a show like he had no idea what was going on. I'd thought for sure he'd reveal the inner workings of his plan, and when he didn't, I started to doubt some of my assumptions. Maybe it wasn't him in the woods. It could have been some other big, bearded guy. With a furtive glance at Helen, I decided, for lack of any other ideas, to say something like the truth. "I had a dream about you," I said.

"A dream," said McTavish, repeating it maybe to highlight how ridiculous it sounded.

"I'm in Longbelly Graveyard," I said, "and so are you."

McTavish's beard completely covered any expression on his face. His little eyes flicked back and forth between me and Helen. On the TV next to him, *The Dead of Night* ended, marking the first time in my whole life I'd failed to watch an episode all the way through. The program switched to the news—a story about the rail strike. There was a close-up of a rail yard, and of some people in suits standing next to a boxcar. I wondered what they were saying, and wished I could be there instead of here.

Finally, McTavish spoke. "I've had that dream too," he said.

I gulped. Now it was going to come out. Helen tensed up next to me.

"I'm in the graveyard," he said, "next to Joseph Brody's grave. I'm sitting on the ground, and I can't move." He paused. "I've had it three nights running. And last night, Henry, you were in it."

"You're . . . paralyzed?" I said.

"Yes," he replied.

"So you didn't bring me there?"

"Bring you?" said McTavish. "We're talking about a dream, Henry." He paused. "Aren't we?" There was real curiosity in his voice.

I didn't know what to say. This conversation was up-ending everything.

"Mr. McTavish," said Helen, "what do you have planned for tomorrow?"

McTavish clearly didn't know what she meant, but I did. "It's circled on your calendar in red," I said.

"You two have had a look around, then," said McTavish.

"We're trying to figure things out," said Helen.

McTavish stood without uttering another word and then returned to the kitchen. I glanced at Helen, but now we were both too curious to run. I heard McTavish rustling the grocery bag, and then he entered carrying a bouquet of flowers. It was beautiful, with lots of little white blooms leading up to six red roses in the middle.

"Who are those for?" Helen asked.

"My wife," said McTavish.

"Is it her birthday?" said Helen.

"No," said McTavish. "The opposite."

I understood then that his wife was dead. "Oh, I'm sorry, sir," I stammered. "When did, um . . ."

"She passed away three years ago," said McTavish. He didn't offer an explanation of how she died, but his voice, when he spoke, sounded much smaller than I'd ever heard it. This guy, who could get a whole class of junior high students to shut up in under two seconds, sounded . . . tiny.

I felt terrible about breaking into McTavish's house while he was getting ready to put flowers on his wife's grave.

"It took me a long time to come back to the world, after she left it," he said. He placed the flowers on the corner table, next to the picture of him and his wife. "It was my work as a teacher that finally helped. And baseball. You have to find those things—the things that connect you to people."

"Is that why you've been trying to help Mr. Dunn?" I asked. "Alan said you want him to start pitching again."

"It's for both of us," said McTavish. He paused, then stepped toward the front door. "You two should get on home," he said. "Henry," he added as he put one hand on the knob, "if you have any more strange dreams, let me know."

"I will," I said.

"And next time you need answers, try asking a few questions first. Save breaking in for later." He opened the door and we stepped through. I think I'd never been so happy to see the sun.

"Um, Mr. McTavish," said Helen, "thank you, sir, for . . . for not killing us."

"You're welcome," said McTavish. He smiled.

You can believe that Helen and I rode fast once we got on our bikes. Helen was thrilled, and when we turned onto our own street, she zigzagged all over. "I can't believe he didn't kill us!" she said, laughing. "I would have killed us for sure."

"Me too," I laughed.

We rolled up our driveway, parked, and went into the house. In the kitchen, the corn chowder was simmering just as I'd left it.

"So, I guess McTavish isn't the one who kidnapped me," I said.

"Or he was lying," said Helen.

"I don't think he was lying," I said.

"If he's really paralyzed, Henry, you could use that. Poke him with a stick or something, until he tells the truth."

"That's what you'd do?" I said.

"Maybe," she said. "Geez, I wish it was me out there, and not you." Her eyes shone with the idea—the adventure of it.

Since the chowder still wasn't quite ready, we went into the living room, where there was still no TV. I picked up the book I'd borrowed from Mrs. Brody, opened it, and started to read, but I didn't get very far. It turned out to be really boring. The text was very dense, in small type, and the first part was about population statistics. I wanted to like it because I liked Mrs. Brody, but there just wasn't anything I could enjoy. I stared a little forlornly at the space where the TV used to be. Then I went upstairs and grabbed *Airman Crusader Versus the Bat Creatures*.

This one started right where *Airman Crusader Versus the Centipede King* had left off. Airman Crusader and the airmen departed from Earth in their galactic cruiser, looking for the potion of immortality on the planet of the bat creatures. When they landed, the planet was all dark, the air ringing with the cries of the rabid bat creatures overhead.

Airman Crusader tied a hook onto some fishing line, cast the line into the sky, and caught a bat creature like a fish. He forced it to reveal the location of the potion.

I dog-eared the page I was on and went to the kitchen to check on the chowder. It was ready.

Helen put out bowls for us. As we ate, she tried once more to convince me to let her rescue me from the grave-yard, but I held firm. I was scared, though, especially as the sun crept past the horizon and the light faded outside.

Just then, the telephone rang. Helen answered, then held the phone out to me. Before I heard the voice on the line, I knew it was Alan, because I could hear the sounds of a baseball game in the background. Alan's dad was watching while Alan talked in the kitchen—almost every conversation I had with him was like this, with people cheering and announcers commentating.

"Henry," said Alan without any preamble, "I'm worried about you. I want us to rescue you tonight."

"But we decided," I said.

"I know," said Alan. "But you could really be in trouble, Henry." He paused. "I mean, maybe you're going to disappear like . . . like Carl."

"We'll find him, Alan," I said. "Maybe I'll learn something useful tonight." I was putting on a show like I wasn't scared, but I was very scared, and Alan's worries were adding to my own.

"Henry, we're just kids," said Alan.

"But Mrs. Brody is helping now," I said, "and aren't the police looking for Carl?"

"Not really," said Alan, bitterly. "They don't care. It's always been like that, even when we lived in Minnesota. Because we're Indians. Carl got in trouble when we were kids all the time, even before he started doing anything wrong. Sometimes I think he got mean just because people expected it."

I didn't really know what to say to this, so I just sat on the line. "Sorry, Henry," Alan said. "I guess I'm just tired of feeling helpless, you know? I want to do something."

"Give me tonight," I said, hoping my voice sounded more confident than I felt. "I'll see what I can find out. Then we'll know enough to be smart."

Suddenly Helen shouted from across the kitchen, "You always want everybody to wait!"

Alan heard her, and laughed. "Okay," he said. "But after tonight, you're going to get help whether you want it or not."

"I'll want it," I said.

We said goodbye and I hung up, but I hadn't taken my hand away before the phone rang again.

"Nilsson residence," I said, putting the receiver to my ear.

"Hi Henry, it's Nicki."

"Oh, er . . . h'lo," I said, making my voice a little lower than normal.

Nicki also requested to come rescue me.

It was nice to have so many concerned friends, that was for sure.

Eventually, minute by minute, it got late. Helen and I brushed our teeth together upstairs. I was wearing my Saturn shirt pajamas, but Helen showed up wearing her nicest pair of jeans with a white belt and a short-sleeved red shirt. Also, she had her earrings in, which she almost never wore—little gold hoops Mom had bought her two years ago.

"Why are you so dressed up?" I said.

"It's what I'll be wearing in the subtle world," said Helen. "And I'm going to meet up with Nicki . . . and Alan." Helen sawed her toothbrush around in her mouth.

"Seriously, Henry, do you think Alan might ask me? I mean, do you think he likes me?"

"I'm sorry, Helen, I just don't know," I said. "I'm a little preoccupied right now."

"It's your own fault for not letting us rescue you," said Helen. She sighed. "Oh Henry, I hope you get out. I'm worried about you, I really am. And I'm also worried about being asked to the dance."

We hugged each other for luck, and went to our rooms.

I got into bed and turned on my radio, softly. It was playing a song by Roy Orbison called "In Dreams." I like Roy Orbison a lot, and think he has a great voice, almost as good as Elvis's. As he sang, I began to count.

CHAPTER 16

IN THE DISTANCE, the branches were singing. My eyes flicked open to find once more the starry sky overhead, with a sliver of moon high above the treetops.

I was in the graveyard, the white sawtoothed trap still clamped onto my leg. I was wearing the same clothes as before — my subtle self hadn't been home to change since it visited here with Mrs. Brody.

And not twenty feet away, I saw the figure from the previous night, the flames from his head lighting the gravestones around him.

"Mr. McTavish," I said. "Can you hear me, sir?"

He didn't respond. He just sat there. The flames leaping from him were the only thing about him that moved, sending up the rainbow of snowflakes. Maybe he could see me right now, but couldn't respond. It seemed likely, since he had no training on how to wake up out of it like I did. Then I saw something I should have noticed before — what McTavish was wearing. He was in a black suit with a white carnation in the buttonhole. It looked familiar, and I remembered seeing him dressed like this at Alan's, just after he'd been to Mr. Brody's funeral.

McTavish shifted, like someone moving in a dream. He stuck out one leg, and there it was—the trap that gripped his ankle—a white, sawtoothed jaw. He'd walked into this in the same way I had.

"Mr. McTavish," I said. "Rock yourself with your eyes. Rock your eyes left and right."

A sound came from farther back, in the woods, back where the headstones gave way to the long black trunks of trees. I saw the familiar flare of firelight. Someone was coming, and the snowflakes that coasted through the branches weren't multicolored—they were white.

I tried to hide, scrambling backwards into the moon shadow of a grave marker, but hiding is more or less impossible when there are rainbows coming out of your head.

The plume of white wound through the trees, closing in, and finally emerged into the graveyard.

It was Carl.

He was wearing the same blue jeans and white T-shirt he had on when I last saw him. He spotted me and started to head my way, but stopped. He looked left and right, and put one hand over his brow to shield out the starlight. I wondered what he was looking for.

The white flakes coming from him disturbed me. I wondered what he'd done to himself to make that happen, to get all white instead of the colors everyone else seemed to have. I didn't know what it meant, but I remembered that when I'd last seen him he'd bragged about it. That cocky kid, though, wasn't the one who came toward me now. He glanced around fearfully, ducking and dodging as if each step might bring down a blow.

When he reached me, he crouched. His eyes were ragged, and his subtle breath shivered in his lungs. "Henry," he whispered, "you gotta help me."

"Carl, what is happening out here?" I said.

He glanced behind, nervously, at no one I could see. "I don't know where I am," he said.

"We're in Longbelly Graveyard."

"No, not that," he said. "Help me, Henry. Help find me." He kind of glared at me as he spoke. It was weird, because he seemed to not care at all that I might need some help too. That I was a prisoner out here, with a jaw trap around my leg.

Again, Carl seemed to think he heard something. He turned toward Mr. Brody's grave, eyes piercing the darkness.

"What is it?" I said.

"They're both out here," he replied. "I don't know where. I don't know . . . I don't know what they want."

"Who, Carl?" I said.

"Abe," said Carl, "and the ghost — the violinist."

CHAPTER 17

I DIDN'T WAKE UP in a great mood when my alarm went off. I got dressed, went down to the kitchen, and ate breakfast with Helen, who was already at the table. Mom and Dad were home, but asleep, and Helen and I got out on our bikes fast so we could discuss what had happened to each of us during the night.

Outside it was cool, and the sky was just turning from dark to light blue. As we pulled away from the house, tires crunching gravel, I wanted to tell Helen that I was now ready to be rescued. But before I could, she said, "Henry, I saw Dad crying."

"What?" I said. "When?"

"Last night when I went downstairs," she said. "Mom and Dad were both home. Mom was in bed, but I heard Dad in the living room, and I went in there, you know, invisibly. He was sitting on the couch. The newspaper was open, but he wasn't reading it. He was looking at where the TV used to be, and . . . and crying."

I tried to imagine this. I'd never, in all my life, seen Dad cry. He was not a crier. He'd been in war, for one thing. I mean, what is there to cry about if you've already been to war? Why would you cry over a lost TV?

We kept pedaling up the road through the wisps of early fog. I was glad it was so nice out, because it kept me from getting even more scared. Things can only be so bad when you and your sister are riding your bikes at sunrise, cool, sweet-smelling air on your face and red-winged blackbirds chatting on the telephone lines.

"Something else," said Helen as we crested a rise. After what she'd already said, I could hardly believe there'd be more.

"What is it?" I asked.

"Alan was kind of dressed up last night. Do you think he was trying to impress me, Henry? Do you think he's going to ask me to the dance?"

I didn't know about that, but I did learn from Helen what the three of them had done that night in their subtle forms—visited a bunch of Carl's hangouts around town, to see if maybe he was ghosting around there. They went to Petersen's Drugstore and Anderssen's Garage, and even out on Stimson Field, a baseball diamond carved into the corn rows on Roy Stimson's land. But no luck. It was eerie.

One minute Carl was giving me a black eye, and the next minute, he vanished. I hoped I was not going to be the next one to disappear.

There was a TV set in homeroom, which was strange. I'd never seen a TV at school before, and for a second I thought maybe it was ours—that Dad had sold it to the district. But it wasn't.

A couple of facility people worked to get it all set up against a wall, while McTavish watched them. It was a big set, and they had to lift it off a utility cart.

Helen and I joined Nicki and Alan. "I've never seen a TV in a class," said Helen to Alan. She batted her eyes at him. That was something else I'd never seen before.

McTavish was looking a little tired. I wondered if having his subtle self trapped in Longbelly Graveyard might be troubling his sleep. Because it was sure troubling mine.

The bell rang, and the facilities people left. McTavish stood, and the class quieted.

"Everyone, you may have noticed the TV in our classroom," he said, joking, since we'd all seen it. "The civil rights march is taking place in Washington today. I know your own families may feel one way or the other, but it's an important piece of American history, and I want us to see it."

McTavish walked over to the set and turned it on. The dot appeared in the middle, grew brighter, and then flared into the biggest gathering I'd ever seen. It was an ocean of people, a whole landscape of them standing in the mall by the Washington Monument—black people and white people.

Things were already under way, because it was an hour later in Washington. I recognized the man who was speaking. He was a church leader from Alabama, Martin Luther King, Jr. I'd seen his picture in the paper. He had one of those voices that was like listening to music. It hypnotized you into paying attention. Even though I didn't know all the words he used, I understood his speech. He said that everyone, all people, have a shared destiny. And for me, what I saw on the screen was an example of that idea, because it was such a huge crowd, all connected by a shared belief.

I glanced at my friends at our little table. I wondered if we were included, in a way, out here in Iowa—part of the destiny Mr. King was talking about. I thought about Carl, lost in the forest somewhere. I thought about Mrs. Brody

in her big house, who'd come here because she was flee-
ing the Nazis before I was born. I thought about my dad
returning home from war and losing his job, and about
Nicki's great-grandfather. I thought about Alan's dad, in
his rundown trailer with his bad back, worrying about his
missing son and watching baseball on TV.

And I felt sure that Mr. King would include all of this, if
he knew about it. That the things he was talking about, in
Georgia and Alabama and Tennessee, were part of things
here in Farro too. He was saying, I thought, that everyone
in the world deserves a chance at life. And deserves help,
if they are in need.

CHAPTER 18

AFTER SCHOOL, THE FOUR OF US met at our bikes. As we pedaled down the road, Alan started to turn left where he'd normally turn right. "See you guys," he said.

"Where're you going, Alan?" I asked.

"Didn't I tell you?" he said. "I got a job, part-time, at Johnson High. Mr. McTavish arranged it with Coach Wilson. I'm going to work in the athletics cage."

"What's the athletics cage?" said Nicki.

As we talked, we circled in the empty intersection.

"The equipment locker," said Alan. "Checking out bats and balls and stuff, and bringing them back in after practice."

"That sounds . . . boring," said Helen.

"It's not so bad," said Alan. "And I'll get to work with Coach Wilson."

"The high school coach," I said.

"Yeah, you know, since I'll probably play for them," said Alan. It was true, and there was no need for him to

pretend humility. He'd be on the varsity team one day —
a great player, like his brother, and like his dad had been.
"Well, I should go," he said, heading off. "Don't worry,
Henry, we'll be there for you tonight." He pedaled away,
his broken spokes clicking.

"And we'll be there for Carl, too," I called after him.

As Helen, Nicki, and I continued along, I said, "Helen, I
wonder if we should get jobs."

"Jobs?"

"To help Mom and Dad," I said. "Get the TV back.
Have you ever thought of having a job, Nicki?" I asked.

"Mom and Dad say school's my job," said Nicki. "That's
why I'm doing the Advanced Humanities program. They
want me to go to college. But Henry, what are you saying — about losing your TV?"

We told her.

When we got home, Mom and Dad were gone. In their
place was a note saying that we (meaning I) should make

dinner. I was happy enough to cook. Even though I was mad at them, knowing that things were hard made me want to help.

As afternoon wore into evening, Helen and I sat in the living room and talked over how I should get rescued.

"You said you can touch the chain and the trap, right?" said Helen.

"Yeah, but I can't break it," I replied.

"Well, if the four of us try together, maybe we can pry it open. I mean, that's a lot more leverage."

"If there is such a thing as leverage in the subtle world," I said. "I'm at least glad that we know where I am." I paused. "You know what?" I said. "I'm surprised I didn't think of this before. When I saw Carl last night, he said, 'Help find me.' Helen, I think he's looking for his body. I mean, his physical body. He's lost out there. He doesn't know where his other half is."

"We looked all over for him last night," said Helen. "Maybe Abe took him away somewhere."

I shivered, though the living room was blazing hot.

CHAPTER 19

AS I RECITED the Fibonacci sequence to myself in bed that night, my mind wandered. I was worried about a lot of stuff, which made it hard to drift off, but strangely the thing that stood out most of all was . . . the color white.

If someone had asked me, a few weeks ago, "What's the first thing you think of when I say the word *white?*" I'd have said snow. And I'd have thought about Christmas and presents and snowball fights and days off from school.

But this impression was changing. Now if someone asked me that same question, I wouldn't think of marshmallows and snowmen. I'd think of the white trap around my ankle. And of the deathly white plume flowing from Carl's head.

I remembered the beginning of the first Airman Crusader story, how Airman Crusader was wearing a white hat. White is a weird color. In some ways, it seems like no color at all. It seems like emptiness.

Slowly, I drifted off. The numbers fuzzed in my head, then continued up along their endless ladder. Now, though, instead of leading me toward a pleasant adventure, they led to a graveyard.

In the distance, I heard the thin creak of branches. I opened my eyes and saw, overhead, the stars shining in a clear sky. I wasn't paralyzed—I guess because I was permanently unzipped from my body now.

I sat up, and saw the hulking shoulders of gravestones all around.

The white teeth of the subtle trap were sunk as firmly as ever into my ankle, the chain still anchored in the ground. Mr. McTavish slumped nearby, cross-legged, eyes open. Maybe he was staring off into whatever dreams his physical body was having—I had no idea. His head was bright with flames, pulsing out a rainbow of subtle snowflakes.

Mine was too. I was a regular bonfire calling to anyone who had any interest in me.

Which someone did.

"Hello there, young man," said a voice, thick with a foreign accent.

I whirled around and backed up to the limit of the chain as a figure emerged from the shadows of a tall grave marker. It was a man dressed in a fine black suit.

He was old, like a grandfather, with a graying mustache that turned upward at the ends. His white shirt collar was high, and a black tie came down from it, and disappeared under a vest. The flames on his head were full and bright, sending up countless colors. In fact, there were more colors than the usual variety. Where I had maybe seven different ones, he had a whole spectrum, with no clear boundary between one shade and another. It was beautiful to behold.

In one hand, he held a violin case.

He watched me curiously, maybe waiting for me to speak. When I didn't, he said, "You're Henry, yes? I believe you know my wife, Maria. My name is Joseph. I'm sorry it has taken me so long." He glanced around cautiously as he approached. "I find that I tire easily, now that I'm dead."

"But h-how . . ." I stammered. That was all I could manage. Seeing a ghost walking around in the graveyard where he was buried didn't put me in a very eloquent frame of mind.

"I'm sure you have questions," said Mr. Brody, "but I must ask mine first. Do you know the name Abe Møller?" As he spoke, he put his violin case flat on the ground and knelt next to it.

"I do," I said.

"Have you seen him?" Mr. Brody asked. "Anytime in the past few days? Either physically or subtly?"

"Carl, my friend's older brother—he was doing something with him out here in the woods," I said. "And," I added, "I have some of his books."

"His science fiction?" said Mr. Brody. I nodded, and he said, "Did you read them?"

"A couple," I said.

Mr. Brody sat down, assuming a sort of conversational posture, as if we were two farmers chatting by the edge of a field. "What did you think? Did you like them? Were they exciting?"

"Pretty exciting," I admitted.

"I wrote books also, with my wife," said Mr. Brody, "but they are not exciting. I've been told they're boring. That's fine with me. But you enjoyed Abraham's books?"

"I . . . I don't know," I said. "I think Airman Crusader wasn't such a good guy."

Mr. Brody nodded. "What has been happening out here in these woods, Henry?" he asked.

I shook my head. "I saw Carl last night. He's scared. I think he's lost his body," I said.

Mr. Brody's good humor evaporated. Very low, he murmured, "It's as I feared."

"What is?" I said.

"There are not many ways to lose your body, Henry," he replied. Just then, across the clearing, McTavish moved in his sleep. Mr. Brody glanced at him. "He wandered in, like you," he observed, "but he has not trained himself to be aware, as you have. Did you read my book on the subject, or learn elsewhere?"

"I read your book," I said.

"Do you know what this is?" he asked, gesturing to the white jaws around my leg.

"It's only here, right?" I said. "It isn't in the real world."

"The real world," Mr. Brody echoed. The term seemed to amuse him. "Did you know, Henry—some people think that the whole universe began in an explosion."

"The Big Bang," I said.

"That's right. The moment before the bang, the universe was a single speck, smaller than a dot of ink. Imagine—everything you see, everyone you know, it all unfolded from that, like a story written out. And so you and I are related to each other, Henry, and even to the stars themselves." He paused. "But I do know what you mean, when you say 'the real world.' You mean the physical world, as opposed to this one we're talking in." Mr. Brody touched the trap on my leg with one hand. "Made of bleach," he murmured, then looked out once more into the forest. "The branches back there sound like a violin, don't you think?" he asked.

"Mr. Brody," I said, "Carl's dead, isn't he? He's . . . a ghost, like you."

"We should not speculate on more than we know," said Mr. Brody. He reached for his violin case and clicked the latches. He opened the case and removed the violin, golden amber in the moonlight, and placed it on the ground. "Henry," he said, "I'd like to help you and your sleeping friend over there. I have with me a key — a subtle key for unlocking a subtle trap. But it will only work once, you understand."

"Help McTavish then," I said, the words sticking in my throat. "He doesn't know what's happening."

"Since you say so, I'll do it." Mr. Brody reached into the case and retrieved a small object, which he held up so I could see it. It was shaped like a house key, but was colored shining black. "I'm afraid you must remain here, Henry." He paused. "You like to read," he said, half to himself, and then a little louder—"Do you like to write? Your own adventure stories?"

"Er, I don't know," I said. "I've never done it."

"Why not?" asked Mr. Brody.

"I don't know," I said. "No one's ever suggested it."

"Well, let me be the first to do so," said Mr. Brody. "The world can use good stories. Especially from critics of *Airman Crusader.*" He reached once more into his violin case, and this time produced a small box. I'm not sure how the box fit in there with the violin, but it did. The box looked like leather. It had a metal clasp on the lid, which was shut. Mr. Brody handed it to me. "Put this on your belt," he said.

I took it. I undid my belt and threaded it through the loops on the back of the case. The box wasn't very big— you could maybe put two sandwiches inside. Once it was fixed, I said, "What's in it?"

"Perhaps a kind of weapon," said Mr. Brody. "Perhaps immortality itself."

I tried to open the lid, but it was shut tight at the clasp, so firm it seemed welded. "Is there a key for it?" I asked.

"Of a sort," said Mr. Brody. "It will open when the time is right." He paused. "One more thing, Henry. Tell me—

can you remember what happens to you here, when you awaken?"

"Yes," I said.

"Then listen. There is a copy of my book on subtle travel, in a bookstore in Farro. Jefferson Used Book and Coin. Do you know that place?"

"Sure," I said, "I go there all the time."

"Open that book," said Mr. Brody. "Find the number inside."

"What number?" I asked.

And then, in an example of very bad timing, I woke up.

I was back in my room. Helen was leaning over me, shaking my shoulders. "Henry," she whispered. "Hey, Henry."

"Blast it, Helen," I said.

"Not my fault," she replied. "Didn't you hear the phone?"

Reflexively, I reached down to my waist to see if the box Mr. Brody had given me was there. It wasn't, of course.

"Mrs. Brody called," said Helen. "She was scared,

Henry. She said someone was in her house—someone broke in."

I glanced at my bedside clock. It was three in the morning.

"Come on, let's go," she said. "We'll get Alan and Nicki on the way."

We dressed and snuck out. We jumped on our bikes, and our generator lights revved up, shining yellow on the pavement. I shivered, because I hadn't put on any kind of jacket and even in summer the middle of the night is cold in Farro.

On the way, I told Helen what had happened—that I'd met Mr. Brody. It was maybe the scariest story I ever told, and even scarier to tell right now, as we raced along pitch-black empty roads.

"Henry, do you believe it, about Carl?" said Helen. "Is he . . . is he dead?"

"I don't know," I replied.

"We shouldn't tell Alan," said Helen. "Not until we're sure."

I didn't want to keep a secret from my best friend, but Helen was right.

We reached the intersection where we had to split

up—Helen to get Nicki, and me to get Alan. We each had our own technique for fetching our best friends at night. Alan was easy—all I had to do was circle around to his bedroom and knock on his window. I guess Nicki was harder, since her bedroom was upstairs, but Helen had managed it plenty of times.

Soon the four of us were biking along South Half, through the maples. I peered across the gulch toward North Half and Longbelly Graveyard. My subtle form was right over there, only a few hundred yards away. And Mr. Brody. And Carl. I glanced at Alan, who was struggling to keep up with us on his half broken bike. I felt terrible for not saying anything about his brother, but I couldn't. Not without being sure.

"There's the lights. She's awake," said Helen, as we rode up.

We parked, went to the door, and knocked. It opened immediately. Mrs. Brody had been standing right there, waiting for us.

"Thank you so much," she said as we entered. "What a terrible night. I've brewed some chamomile tea."

CHAPTER 20

MRS. BRODY COULDN'T tell us much. A sound had awakened her, and she came into the living room to find that someone had slipped inside through the sliding-glass door and searched through the bookcases. The books now lay on the floor in disarray. The intruder must have left when they heard Mrs. Brody coming down the stairs.

"What do you think they wanted?" I asked.

"I've no idea," said Mrs. Brody. "Nothing in my library has much value."

"It must have been Møller," said Helen. "I mean, he had Carl spying on this house. He set up subtle traps around your husband's grave. Now he's going through your books. He's looking for something."

"You guys," I said, "I think . . . I think I know what it is."

All eyes turned to me, and I told the story of what had just happened to me in the graveyard—meeting Mr. Brody and receiving the case, which I'd threaded onto my belt.

"I knew I'd seen him," said Mrs. Brody, when I finished. Her eyes shone.

"You guys," I said, "do you remember, the day Carl beat us up, what he said right as he left?"

No one did.

"He said, 'I'm gonna live forever.' And that was in the Airman Crusader books — the airmen were trying to get the secret of immortality. And . . . I think maybe Mr. Brody just gave it to me."

"I don't understand," said Helen.

"The secret," I said. "That's what's in the case. Mr. Brody said . . . that it was a weapon, and it was immortality."

"But it's locked, Henry?" said Nicki.

"Yeah, for now," I said. Then I told the rest too, about the copy of *Subtle Travel* at Jefferson Used Book and Coin. "There's a number in it," I said.

"What kind of number?" said Alan.

"I don't know," I said. "That's when my sister woke me up."

"Not my fault," said Helen.

We stayed with Mrs. Brody until morning—fortunately, Mom and Dad always slept in after a late shift, and wouldn't know we'd been gone.

Helen, Alan, and I were in favor of skipping school and going straight to the bookstore, but Nicki wouldn't have it. She absolutely would not miss class. "That place doesn't open until nine," she said. "Let's go during lunch break."

"Seems like a good idea," I said, happy to be on her side.

Jefferson Used Book and Coin was in the old part of North Farro, between Sam's Barbershop and Fresh Town Market Deli. The owner, Mr. Clemens, was a friendly man with wiry black hair that he combed over a bald spot. When the four of us arrived on our bikes he was outside, just unlocking the front door, with a paper bag in one hand that I knew contained a hamburger from Fresh Town (because I'd been here during lunch in the past and seen similar bags). Clemens heard us behind him as we dropped our kickstands.

"Good afternoon," he said. "The Nilsson Twins, Nicki Chen, and Alan Dunn." He nodded to each of us as he said our names. Farro was a small town, and he knew us all.

"We're trying to find a book, Mr. Clemens," I said.

"I have some of those," said Mr. Clemens. (He always made this joke.) Then he said, "You look like you got poked with the wrong end of a stick, Henry."

He ushered us inside. The midday sun was blazing and the little shop was hot. It was jammed with books, many of which were not on shelves, but were stacked next to shelves in towers. The place was confusing, but I'd always liked it, and I thought Mr. Clemens was a nice guy.

He stepped behind the front counter, which was a glass display full of money—new and old, domestic and foreign.

"What's the title of your book?" he asked, putting his lunch bag on the counter.

"*Subtle Travel and the Subtle Self*," I said.

"Oh, that's odd," said Mr. Clemens.

"Odd, sir?" I said.

"Someone else called me about it this morning. Said he'd heard I had a copy. But I checked, and no. Of course," he said, waving one hand around at the disorganized shop, "I explained that sometimes things evade me. He said he might come by and have a look himself. He was quite insistent."

I was stunned. "He was listening in," I whispered. It was Abe—it had to be. He'd been in the forest. He'd overheard my conversation with Mr. Brody. For some reason, he wanted to get to that book before we did.

"Spirituality is the last row at the back," said Mr. Clemens.

We dove into the shop.

When we were far enough in to be out of earshot of Mr. Clemens, I said, "I think Møller was listening last night, when I talked to Mr. Brody. Now he's headed here!"

"Let's hurry," said Alan.

Mr. Clemens's store was a mess. It looked like a tornado had passed through without finding the book it wanted. Eventually we reached a handwritten faded sign that said "Spirituality," next to the back windows.

We looked in the alphabetical position where the book should be, first for Møller and then for Brody, but it wasn't in either spot.

"Let's just scan the whole case," said Helen. She and Alan started at the top and worked their way down while Nicki and I started at the bottom and worked up. As we converged at the center, we all spotted it at once. It was tough to see because the spine was so sun-faded. I pulled it out.

This copy was in better condition than the one from the woods, and I thought it had probably been right here for years. I opened to the title page and saw the names of the authors — and then saw something different. Near the bottom, someone had impressed an ink stamp, in blue. It showed a horizontal human body, and out of that another body rising, depicted with a dotted line.

"It's a subtle form," said Nicki.

Below this image were five bold letters, like an acronym: NFTSA, followed by the number Joseph Brody had told me about. "A telephone number," I said.

"Should we buy this?" said Alan. He pointed to the price penciled on the inside cover — twenty-five cents.

Well, Nicki had a dime, but that was all we could scrounge up. "We can't let Møller find it," I said.

"Henry Nilsson," said Helen, snorting in amusement, "are you suggesting what I think you are?"

"I . . . I am suggesting that, yes," I stammered.

"Don't you think we should make a pros and cons list first?" she said, poking me playfully.

"You're good at this, Helen," I said. "How should we do it?"

"Give it here," she said. I handed her the book and she stuck it under her shirt, jammed it inside the waistband of her jeans. To me this seemed kind of obvious, but I guess obviousness is not as important as confidence when it comes to theft.

We returned to the front of the store.

"Did you find it?" said Mr. Clemens.

"I don't think you have it," I said. "That guy will be disappointed."

Helen was already leaping out through the front door, but I hesitated. Something caught my eye — a piece of paper taped to the front of the glass display cabinet. It read, "Part Time Help Wanted."

"Mr. Clemens, are you hiring someone?" I asked.

"For weekends, to do some organizing," he said. "You may have noticed a few things out of place . . ." He smiled.

"Could I have an application?" I asked. I thought maybe I'd work an hour or two for free to start, as a way of paying for the book we'd just stolen.

He squinted at me. "I don't see why not," he said, "except that there is no application. That's how disorganized I am. Tell me, do you think you're the man for the job?" He studied me. "Old Man Clemens and One-eye Nilsson?"

"Oh, nobody calls me that," I said. "They call me —"

"HEN-REE!" Helen shouted from outside.

We hopped on our bikes and sped up the street toward the nearest pay phone, but we hadn't gone more than a few yards before I brought my bike up short.

"Wait a second, you guys," I said. I gestured to the corner of a nearby building, which looked like a decent hiding spot. "If he's coming here — Møller — I want to see him."

"Lunch is ending," said Nicki. "And we don't have any idea when he'll arrive."

"Come on, guys," I said. "Stake it out with me."

My friends agreed, but our surveillance only lasted about two minutes before Helen got fed up and Nicki started glancing back toward school.

"Henry," said Alan, "I want to see him too, but maybe we should get to the phone."

"Okay, you're right," I said, sighing.

We unstaked and pushed our bikes up the block.

"What were you talking to Clemens about, Henry?" said Helen as we closed in on the phone booth.

"He's hiring someone," I said. "I think I applied."

"A job?" said Helen.

"To help Mom and Dad," I said. "Get our TV back."

We parked our bikes next to the booth and crammed inside, closing the double-hinged door behind it. It was a tight fit, and Nicki and I ended up almost cheek to cheek.

"Make the call," said Helen. "I can smell your armpits, Henry."

"You are smelling your own armpits," I replied. I picked up the receiver. Nicki dropped her dime in the slot, and I dialed the number in the book after Helen took it out from under her shirt. I always hate dialing zero when I'm in a hurry, because it takes so long to circle around—and Helen hates it even more. "Go, go, go," she chanted as the dial turned. We all pressed our ears close to the receiver and waited breathlessly as it rang once, twice. Then I heard a click. Someone had picked up on the other end.

A woman's voice echoed as if it was coming from the end of a long hall. "You have reached NFTSA," she said. "Dial 1 for remote reset."

"Hello?" I said. "My name is Henry Nilsson."

"You have reached NFTSA," the voice repeated. "Dial 1 for remote reset."

"It's a recording," said Helen.

"Should I dial 1?" I asked.

"Geez, Henry!" said Helen, fed up with my hesitation.

Well, okay then. I put my finger into the hole and turned the dial. A beep sounded, then a sudden rush of sound came on the line, like hundreds of people applauding.

With a click, the sound was cut off.

"They hung up!" said Helen, incensed, as the dial tone returned.

"Does anyone have another dime?" I asked, but no one did.

I placed the receiver in the cradle, and saw that the hairs on my arm were standing up.

We piled out of the booth and went to our bikes. As I was throwing my leg over the top bar, though, I saw something.

"Look," I said, pointing across the street at the strip by the bookstore.

There was a car parked out front—a white Chevy that hadn't been there before. I peered at the store's front windows. Inside, through the gleam on the glass, I could see someone moving around.

"It's him," I whispered.

The figure stepped up to the windows.

And we saw him, though not clearly.

He was pretty old, maybe in his seventies, tall, and wore a white short-sleeved shirt and white pants. His face looked tired, but even at this distance I could pick up an unnerving intensity in his gaze.

He was looking right at us, and behind us—at the telephone booth.

He knew what we'd just done.

We jumped on our bikes and rushed off, pedaling for all we were worth.

CHAPTER 21

AFTER SCHOOL, WE RECONVENED at the bike racks. Alan had to go to work, and the rest of us decided to tag along so we could talk. Of course Helen and I were still officially grounded, and I knew Mom and Dad would be home today, waiting for us.

"I don't care," said Helen, when I mentioned it. "Let them get mad. They're wrong!"

Normally I'd have wanted to go along with the grounding, to give things time to cool, but the situation being what it was, and our punishment being so unfair, I found myself in agreement with my sister.

"It's fine if you guys want to come," said Alan. "I'm not really working today, anyway. There's some off-season ball with the JV team out at Stimson Field. Coach invited me to play."

"To play with the JV high-schoolers?" I said.

"Yeah," said Alan. He didn't sound very excited. At any other time he would have been thrilled, but I could see he was worrying about his brother. The longer Carl remained missing, the more awful the whole thing seemed.

Stimson Field was well known around town. The diamond was a little smaller than regulation, but nicely limed, with real bases and a pitcher's mound bordered on three sides by the field and on one side by the road. The JV players and Coach Wilson were there when we arrived, and Coach beckoned Alan over. Helen, Nicki, and I sat on some old wooden bleachers nearby.

"Don't lead off the base so much!" Helen shouted at a player. She didn't play baseball much herself, but she knew all about it. She was good at every sport. Right after she yelled, the player she'd criticized was thrown out. Then Alan was up.

He swung at the first pitch and connected with a bullet-like drive that bounced fast across the outfield and disappeared into the cornstalks. The center fielder went in after it as Alan slowly rounded the bases. He walked a little. He jogged. Then he jogged backwards. The other players laughed.

He approached home, and still the ball he'd whacked

hadn't been found. He slowed before crossing the plate, then stopped and turned toward the cornfield, where the other outfielders were heading to search for the ball.

Then he jogged in that direction, presumably to help look.

Alan had been my best friend for quite a while. Years. And sometimes I felt I knew him as well as I knew anyone. This was one of those times. I saw that his pace wasn't casual, as if he was simply going to look for a ball. He ran the way you do when you're afraid you've lost something important.

I stood up in the bleachers.

"What is it, Henry?" said Helen.

"Nothing," I said, and I was off like a shot after Alan.

Among the rows of corn, I heard a few players rummaging around even as Coach Wilson bellowed from a distance that we should stop looking for the ball—there were plenty of others.

I jogged up one row, but then heard someone's footsteps in the next row over. I pushed through and found myself a few yards behind Alan, who'd just come to a stop. He was staring straight ahead, at nothing.

I came up next to him, and waited. I knew he would speak.

"No one cares," he said after a moment.

"It's not true, Alan," I said. "We all care. We'll find him, I know we will."

"I know you don't like him," said Alan. "I don't blame you, Henry. Sometimes I don't like him either." He paused, still staring off down the row. "But you have to understand. He raised me, as much as anyone did, after Mom left, and Dad was playing ball and traveling. He put me to bed at night. He cooked. Hell, he taught me to read, Henry." Alan fell silent. I put a hand on his shoulder. I remembered what Mr. Brody had told me, in the graveyard, about everyone being related because we all came out of the Big Bang. It felt kind of like that now. Someone had gone missing, and everyone was affected by it.

Then I heard a sound behind us, and turned to see Helen and Nicki emerge. They came up to us without speaking, and we all hugged in a group.

Helen leaned forward with a laugh and tipped us over, and we collapsed into a friendly pile.

Suddenly Nicki exclaimed, "There it is!" She reached out and plucked the missing ball from the cornstalks.

When Helen and I finally rolled up to the house on our bikes, Mom and Dad were waiting, as we knew they would be, sitting at the kitchen table and fuming over our absence. They were in their work clothes, getting ready to leave.

"Look what the cat dragged in," said Dad icily as we entered.

"You both," said Mom, "are in big trouble."

"That's what you think," said Helen, suddenly charging past me. Wow, my twin sister—she never stops. She reached into her back pocket and produced a piece of paper, which she smacked down on the kitchen table. "If you can't take care of us," she said loudly, "we'll take care of ourselves."

I had no idea what this was about. Mom and Dad looked at the paper, and then at Helen, who said, "I got a job, and Henry got one too—at Jefferson Used Book and Coin. He's starting this weekend."

Of course, this wasn't totally true . . . but it was kind of true. I craned my neck to get a look at Helen's piece of paper. It was a pay stub from Marlon's Pizza Pies in downtown Farro. My brain spun. Helen? Pizza pies?

"Is this true, Henry?" said Mom.

"Yes," I said.

No one spoke for a few seconds.

Then, slowly, Dad put both of his hands palm down on the table. He looked between them, where his thumbs were almost touching. "There was a guy I knew," he said.

I'm not sure how I could tell, but I was certain that Dad was going to say something about the war. My heart thudded. Next to me, Helen took a deep breath. She'd asked Dad about Korea tons of times, but he'd never said anything.

"Name of Davis," Dad said now, mumbling a little, as if he wasn't talking to us, but just to himself. "Private first class." He kept his eyes on the space between his hands. "We were in the city, and it was getting dark. Then I heard shots. We ran. Took cover in an alley. But Davis wasn't with us. He was behind, around the corner, and I saw him. Lying out there on his back, in the street. And making a sound, like gargling. Like gargling before bed, like a Listerine ad, because they shot him . . . in the throat." Dad paused. He took a breath. "We wanted to go get him, but we couldn't move from cover. They were pounding us, sniper fire, automatic fire, artillery. Then the North Koreans . . . they went up to Davis. And I watched . . . as they . . . they stripped him. They took his gun, his belt. Jacket. Helmet. Boots. Right off him, while he was still trying to breathe. They took everything. And they left him there, naked in the street. He died there." Dad brought his hands together on the tabletop, lacing his fingers, like the curtains closing at the end of a play.

"I never thought I'd see that again," he said slowly. "Taking everything from a man while he's still living. But here it is. Right here in my own home, it's happening." His eyes had gone glassy, and he wiped them with his sleeve. Then he stood, turned crisply as if he were on the parade field, and walked out the kitchen door, letting the screen slap closed behind him.

Mom was just as startled as we were, I think. She wiped her own eyes, and gestured to the chairs opposite her at the kitchen table. Helen and I sat wordlessly.

"You're good kids," she said. "You didn't have to do this. We'll get by."

Helen had started this off, and I felt it was up to me to finish it. "You guys are wrong about Nicki and Alan," I said. I didn't provide any reason why this was true. I just said it, as if it had been established in court.

Mom nodded. "Tonight is your father's last shift at the yard," she said. "Please, both of you, go easy on him. He's struggling."

"We're struggling too," said Helen.

"I know," said Mom. She paused. "Henry, will you make dinner? I bought ingredients for three-bean soup."

"I will," I said.

Mom stood, and followed Dad out. Within thirty seconds, the car backed out of the driveway and disappeared up the road.

I turned to Helen. I saw her eyes were red—I think not so much from Dad's story, as from the fact that he'd told it. After all of this time, he'd finally trusted us with something that happened to him in the war. I'm sure my eyes were red too. "You . . . you have a job?" I asked.

"Of course not," said Helen, sniffling, but smiling at what a dummy I was. "I found that in the trash at school."

I shook my head in wonder. She had no fear.

I started on dinner. I made a salad with shredded carrots, apples, raisins, sliced almonds, and mayonnaise. I made three-bean soup. As I was sifting flour for blueberry muffins, Helen entered and said, "You're going to town in here."

"Trying to keep my mind off things," I said.

"Don't worry, Henry—we'll rescue you tonight," she said, and she kept me company after that.

Eventually, it was bedtime. We got into our pajamas and met in the bathroom to brush our teeth. Helen was all dressed up again in nice jeans and her favorite red shirt, hoping to impress Alan with her subtle form. I noticed that she'd put on some of Mom's lipstick.

"Do you want me to stay in your room, Henry?" she asked. "I could bring in my sleeping bag."

"No, it's okay," I said.

We hugged in the hall and I went into my room. I got into bed, propped up my arm, and started counting, but I couldn't stay focused. There were too many other thoughts breaking in.

I stood and went to my desk, and got pencil and paper. Before, whenever I'd written things down, it was because I wanted to change something that had happened. But this time I wrote things down as they were, or as near as I could. I wasn't trying to change anything. I was trying, with all I had in me, to understand. The pencil seemed to move of its own accord—Møller, Carl, the graveyard, Airman Crusader, the ghost of Joseph Brody, my dad

. . . even my fears about the Fall Formal flowed onto the page.

And amazingly, I started to relax. My mind cleared. I felt calm enough to lie down again. Maybe that's one reason people write — to have a place to put everything so you can get some sleep.

CHAPTER 22

I HEARD A LONG NOTE, and right away thought it was those branches sawing behind the graveyard. But when I listened again, it didn't sound quite like that. It was a voice—a human voice. Someone was singing. I opened my subtle eyes and saw not stars above me and gravestones all around, but my ceiling, and my bedroom. A few colorful snowflakes wafted by.

On the radio, Elvis performed the last lines of "Are You Lonesome Tonight?" and the station went off the air. I lay listening to the static. I could hardly believe it. I was home.

I was once more stuck in the paralysis, and was about to start rocking myself out of my body when a voice spoke, off to my left.

"You have quite a way with words," it said. I recognized it instantly, just like before. It was raspy and quiet. At this point I didn't have any doubts that my midnight visitor was Abe Møller.

I rolled my eyes around until I caught sight of him, standing over by my desk. He was looking at the sheets I'd written before I fell asleep—my whole analysis of the situation.

"Don't read that," I said.

"Not to worry, young man," came the reply, "there's nothing new here for me, except to discover what a fine writer you are. You should develop your gift. The written word is a powerful thing. Did you know that books create their own flux streams? Fascinating."

Møller's tone of voice was friendly in a way, but the affability stuck to the surface, like the frozen top of a lake.

He moved away from my desk and came closer. As before, I could make out that he was wearing a set of blue-striped pajamas and what looked like a white hat.

Then I noticed something new, or rather, something missing. I didn't see any flakes coming from him—neither rainbow flakes nor white ones. There were no pale flames licking up either. I badly wished I could turn my head to get a better look.

"I think we decided last time," said Møller, "that you might ask me a question next we met. Have you got one?"

I did. It was the question that lay beneath this whole adventure, really—the single thing that had set it all in motion. I didn't expect Møller to give me a straight answer, but it wouldn't hurt to try.

"Did you kill Carl?" I said.

"Hmm," said Møller, meditatively. "It's unfortunate that you called the number you found in that book, young man. Now we may never properly know what has happened to Carl. You've forced me to rush things." He didn't sound angry about this, but was very matter-of-fact. "I overheard you, of course, in the graveyard with Joseph, talking about the Big Bang last night."

"I knew you were listening," I said.

"Let me explain properly to you," said Møller, "what Joseph did not. Before our universe began, Henry, everything was a single point of light—a perfect white dot. This point exploded outward into creation. Joseph thinks this was a good thing, but he's wrong. The universe is degenerating, Henry. For instance, did you know that mankind was originally a white race? The first men were white, and only over time devolved into the colors we have now—red, yellow, brown. Likewise with the rainbow of flakes that comes from your skull, which is called a flux stream—did you know that babies produce only white? Through life, this perfection is lost. We grow weak and die." He paused, and stepped toward my window to look outside, which took him fully out of my range of vision.

"What does it mean to you to be a good person?" he said. "Before you answer, let me tell you what it means to me. For me, goodness requires that I resist death, both for my own sake and also for the sake of all men. I believe we have spirits that can survive forever, if we learn the way. That discovery will be my great gift—to myself, and to all mankind. Now you tell me, Henry, what does it mean to be good?"

Well, I just can't answer that kind of question on the spot. So instead of answering, I said, "What do you want? Why are you here?"

Møller nodded, accepting that I wouldn't answer. "It's simple. I want the box that Joseph gave you. And in the service of goodness, I'm prepared to take it, whether you give it to me or not."

For a moment I was kind of glad to be paralyzed. I think it kept me from acting as scared as I was. And because I couldn't move or run or do much of anything, I remembered a great piece of advice I'd gotten not that long ago, from my twin sister. "Yell for me," she'd said. "I'm right down the hall." I took a deep breath and called out with all I had in me: "Helen-n-n! Hel-l-l-p!" My subtle voice rang through my room and, I hoped, through the whole house.

"I'll see you soon, Henry," Møller said, calmly. "When you want to find me, I'll be in the graveyard."

"Why would I want to find you?" I asked. But I received no reply. Møller was gone, as fast as last time, vanished into thin air.

Then another voice sounded. It was a man's voice, coming in through my window from outside, down by the front of the house. "Hello up there — is everything all right?"

I didn't think everything was all right, but since I didn't know who was asking, I didn't reply. Instead, I calmed myself as best I could and began moving my eyes back and forth, sloshing myself out of my stuck body. Soon, thankfully, I made the tip and found myself lying face down on the floor.

I stood and looked at my body in bed, left arm resting where it had fallen. I seemed unharmed. I went to the closet mirror and examined my subtle form. Everything was as it should be. There I was in my Saturn shirt and blue pajama pants. There was no white jaw clamped to my leg. One thing was different, though — at my waist was the leather box Mr. Brody had given me. It was integrated with my new outfit. Instead of being secured to the leather belt on my jeans, it was now attached to the drawstring of my pajama pants.

"Are you all right up there?" said the voice from outside. I snuck up to the window from beneath, and peeked carefully out.

There was a man below, pulsing multicolor flakes up into the night. He was a black man. He wore some kind of uniform — a green jacket with epaulets, tough pants with perfect creases, and black patent leather shoes. He held a clipboard and a pen. At his side was a large square case, hung from his shoulder by a strap.

I hesitated. I'd just gotten out of a bad jam, and wasn't overeager to leap into the next one. However, something occurred to me. I'd yelled to my sister for help, and she had not arrived.

My heart thudded in my chest as Møller's final words came back to me. I rushed into the hall, to Helen's room, ghosted through her door, and approached her bed.

She lay atop her covers, wearing the yellow sundress Mom had gotten her last spring. I guessed she'd put it on for Alan's sake — still hoping he'd ask her to the dance.

But more important than any of this, her body was empty. Her subtle self was not in it, or anywhere in the room.

Because she had gone out—out to the graveyard to rescue me. She, and Alan and Nicki.

I took a deep breath, trying to compose myself as I came to grips with the situation. My friends would not be rescuing me tonight, as we'd planned. No. I would be rescuing them.

I put one hand on the box at my waist. Mr. Brody had said it contained the secret to immortality—what Møller had been searching for. But he also said it was a weapon. I only hoped it would unlock at the right moment.

"Do you need help?" said the man from outside, his voice ascending through Helen's open window.

I went downstairs. I paused before the front door, scared. I had no idea what was about to happen. I only knew that my friends were in danger, and now was not the time to sit around debating the pros and cons. I tried to imagine Helen charging forward, full of certainty, responding as the situation demanded.

I stepped through the door.

The man was standing on the front drive. He still had the big case hanging from a strap at his shoulder, and his clipboard and notepad in hand. "Are you Henry Nilsson?" he asked as I appeared.

"That's right," I said. He had a neat mustache and a large jaw. I noticed right away that he didn't seem unfriendly. He was the first black person I had ever talked to. "I have three other names," he said, glancing at his clipboard. "Helen Nilsson, Nicki Chen, and Alan Dunn. Are they here?"

"They need help," I said. I paused and then, trying to sound authoritative, added, "Who are you?"

"Sergeant Ray Johnson, at your service," said the man. "NFTSA."

As he said it, I saw the insignia above his left breast pocket — the exact same as the blue stamp in the used book. "The stamp!" I exclaimed. "What is that? What does it mean?"

Sergeant Johnson looked surprised. "*You* called *us*," he said. "Where did you find the number? In a marked book?"

"It was in the *Subtle Travel* book," I said, "at Jefferson Used Book and Coin. But Sergeant, what did it mean? What happened when I dialed the number?"

"The acronym," he said , indicating the patch on his pocket, "stands for National Flux Travel Security Administration. You dialed our remote reset call-in number, which caused two things to happen. First, it replaced your subtle form into your physical body. Second, it located you and flagged you as an undocumented flux traveler."

"I . . . I don't understand," I said, simultaneously looking up the dark road. I didn't have all night to stand here talking. "Sergeant," I said, "there's an emergency."

"All right," he replied, "but first, I have something to give you." He reached into a pocket and retrieved a small card that looked like a library card, and handed it to me. On the face side it showed the emblem we'd seen stamped in the book—the human form rising out of itself. The other side was printed with information.

"OFFICIAL USFT PASSPORT FOR HENRY L. NILSSON," it read. (My middle name is Leo.) Next to this were my birth date, my address, and my social security number.

"Everything spelled correctly?" asked Sergeant Johnson.

"Yes," I said. "But what is it?"

"NFTSA is a government organization that exists here on the flux plane," he replied. "What the Brody-Møller book calls the subtle plane. We regulate flux travel within the borders of the United States. Keep your passport on your person at all times," he said, moving into what sounded like a set speech. "If asked for it by any representative of NFTSA or other recognized government flux agency, you must provide it. Every citizen of the United States has the right to travel, but every flux traveler must register with NFTSA and keep their registration current. Do you understand these rights and responsibilities?"

I nodded. It was a lot to take in — the subtle plane had always seemed like a place for only me and my friends. Discovering that there was a whole federal agency in charge of it was a big shift. But it made sense. I mean, if there were books about how to do all of this, why wouldn't people know about it?

"Don't be nervous," said the sergeant. "This is standard protocol. Now, regarding your emergency . . ."

"I'll tell you on the way," I said, already walking out toward the road. "Have you ever heard of a man named Abe Møller?"

Sergeant Johnson stopped in his tracks. "Henry," he said, "you need to tell me what you're getting us into. Now." His voice was quiet, intense.

"So you have heard of him," I said. "He's been out in the woods here. I think he just kidnapped my friends, and he might have killed my best friend's brother, Carl." That seemed to cover it. Then I added, "And he's been spying on Joseph Brody."

This last fact seemed to newly alarm the already-startled sergeant. "Joseph Brody?" he said. "But I have a report that he died . . ." he started flipping through some of the paperwork on his clipboard.

"He did die," I said, "but he survived it."

Despite holding his clipboard at the ready, the sergeant had written nothing. Now he put the cap back on his pen. He took the square case from his side and laid it on the ground. "Excuse me," he said. He unlatched the top of the case, opened it, and took out a telephone, whose wire went down inside the case. He held the receiver to his ear and dialed. "Sergeant Johnson for Colonel Dattilo," he said. He paused a moment, then continued. "Colonel, we have a situation. I have report on Abe Møller in . . ." he paused, then said to me, "This town is called Farro?"

"That's correct, sir," I said.

"Farro, Iowa," he said into the phone.

The voice on the other end spoke briefly, and by its tone, I took the remark to be something along the lines of "That is impossible, Sergeant, you must be mistaken."

"Sir, the report is clear. The witness is with me now.

Furthermore, he claims that Joseph Brody, that is *the* Joseph Brody, the author . . . that he has achieved posthumous coherence."

This time the voice on the phone spoke longer.

"Yes, sir," said Sergeant Johnson, and then, "Understood." He put the phone back, closed up the case, and shouldered it again. "We're going to have to do our best for the moment, Henry," he said, sizing me up as you might a newly conscripted deputy. "My unit will send backup, but they need to fall asleep and then transport here. It will take some time. If we can find Møller, and keep him within sight for long enough . . . well, we might just have a chance of apprehending him." Sergeant Johnson took in a deep breath and let it out slowly. He was afraid.

CHAPTER 23

THE SUBTLE NIGHT wasn't the same as the regular night. There were different sounds, and my subtle eyes could see everything, even though all the shapes were black. Also, the sergeant and I each had our own personal torch in the form of our blazing heads, which cast flickering reddish shadows on fence posts, trees, and up the road as we headed out the highway toward the turnoff for North Half.

"So, Henry, tell me what's been happening," said the sergeant.

"If you don't mind, I'd like to ask you a couple of questions first," I said. "Everyone keeps asking me things, and never telling me anything. But I need to know: Who is Abe Møller?"

"He's the most wanted criminal in the U.S. flux plane," replied Sergeant Johnson. "He has committed countless crimes in the name of research, for years. And has evaded us at every turn."

"What is flux? I heard Møller use that word, too."

"Sorry. I'm not used to explaining these things to civilians. Abe Møller is a scientist who has a particular research specialty—a substance known as *fluxus achromia*." The sergeant gestured upward, at the flames and snowflakes above us. "These are flux streams," he said. "The colors, hues, and shapes differ somewhat from person to person, as they're the result of our mental activity."

"Is it our thoughts?" I asked.

"We don't really know," he replied. "Part of it seems to be thoughts or intentions or beliefs, but our ideas about this are largely speculation."

"So, if this is flux, what's *fluxus achromia*?" I asked.

"It's white in color," said the sergeant. "Sometimes it's called bleach. You might say that it's empty—whatever it is that gives color to a flux stream is absent from the bleach. And while we can't say much about the meaning of the various colors of flux, we have learned a thing or two about bleach." He paused. "Everywhere we've found it, we've also found . . . cruelty."

I thought of Carl's disappearance, and of my friends who were now out in the woods with Abe Møller, and I picked up the pace a little. "When Mrs. Brody talked about him," I said, "she talked about contempt. About people who don't care who they hurt."

"Henry," said the sergeant, "you're sure you really saw him—Joseph Brody—after his death? With your own eyes? Spoke to him?"

I didn't reply. The highway bent before us off to the right at the turnoff for North Half. The trees came up thickly on both sides, and the black, narrow dirt lane snaked ominously off into the woods.

"Sergeant," I said, "this is the turnoff. The graveyard isn't far."

"Well, Henry, now it's your turn," he replied. "What do I need to know before we go in there?"

"That my friends are in trouble," I said. I paused, then gestured to the waist of my pajama pants, at the leather box. "Mr. Brody gave me this," I said. "He said it contains the key to immortality. Abe Møller wants it. But Mr. Brody also said whatever is in here . . . is some kind of weapon."

"You haven't opened it?" asked Sergeant Johnson.

"It's locked, sir. Mr. Brody said it will open when the

time is right." I paused. "I think when I called you, it interrupted whatever Møller was trying to do to Carl. He was experimenting on him, trying to get him to survive dying. 'Posthumous coherence,' I heard you say. That's what he wants—to be immortal. Maybe he failed with Carl, I don't know. But I think he needs to take this box from me to finish what he started."

The sergeant frowned, which did not fill me with confidence. But we had to keep going.

The forest pressed in on us once we turned alongside the gorge. The black trunks of the maple trees cluttered the darkness, and everything felt very close.

"Henry," said Sergeant Johnson, his voice low, "you said you talked to Joseph Brody out here. What did he say?"

"He had a key for opening one of the traps," I said. "And we decided he'd free Mr. McTavish, my teacher, who was also trapped." I paused. "Møller set those to try to catch Mr. Brody, didn't he?"

"Probably," said the sergeant, "but when he caught you instead, he simply monitored the situation. What kind of key did Mr. Brody have, Henry? Did you see it?"

"It looked like a regular house key," I said.

"What color?"

"Black." When the sergeant didn't reply, I turned to find him staring at me.

"Maybe it appeared black, in the darkness," he said. "But it's actually some other color."

"No, it was black," I said. "Black as tar."

The sergeant looked for a moment like he was going to stop and use his field telephone again, but he just shook his head. "If you're correct, Henry, you may be the first person to have ever seen *fluxus polychromia* — black flux, which is sometimes called ink."

"Poly . . . that's many, right?" I said. "So is it the opposite of the bleach?"

Sergeant Johnson nodded. "Ink has never been observed," he said, "but we've theorized about it. The opposing quality to the bleach."

"So if the bleach is about cruelty," I said, "then ink would be about . . . um, kindness?"

"*Understanding* would be a better term," said the sergeant. "You see, the colors of our flux streams indicate connections. We don't know what they mean, but we do know they show our connection to other people, ideas, emotions, beliefs. This is what the bleach lacks. It is unaffiliated. It rejects, refuses. It is cruel. The ink, on the other hand, represents an equally powerful connection—an understanding."

We reached the sign for Longbelly Graveyard. In the distance, I heard the two branches scraping, the lonely voice of the forest, which never rested.

CHAPTER 24

WE WERE ONLY about twenty yards off from the graveyard. It was a little hard to navigate—even though we could both see in the dark, the closeness of the trees to the narrow road was disorienting.

We passed through the gate and I could see, far inside in the midst of the hundreds of standing gravestones, rainbow snowflakes—my friends, I thought. I started to rush forward, but the sergeant put one hand on my shoulder. "Wait," he said. He was right. We had no idea what the situation was. We didn't know if—

Sergeant Johnson stumbled and fell, dropping his clipboard and the case that contained his field phone.

Clamped to his leg was the white jaw of a bleach trap, the teeth firmly fixed.

"Henry," said the sergeant urgently, "open your box."

I reached to my waist and pulled the flap, but it wouldn't budge. "Go—sneak behind, through the forest," the sergeant hissed. "Try to open it again. I'll distract him if I can."

I was glad the sergeant didn't panic, because I was ready to. Maybe they teach you in the military to be calm under fire, or maybe he just had the right personality. Whatever the reason for his self-control, I thankfully took his advice.

I dodged away into the forest. As soon as I was clear of the sergeant I heard him shout, "Abraham, it's Johnson here. Come out. I'm trapped, I can't hurt you. I want to talk." The salutation was so familiar, it made me wonder how long the sergeant had been after Møller. Maybe a long time.

I headed quickly through the darkness into the forest, and the trees closed in around me, obscuring (I hoped) the bright flag of my spectral flux. I considered rushing to my friends, who I was sure were in peril, but I hesitated. I wasn't sure what to do, and it was horrible. It was all up to me.

I moved much faster than I could have run in my real body, because I didn't have to go around trees—I went straight through them, glimpsing the concentric rings and the center pole of heartwood, smelling the sap, then pressing on.

When I thought I was safely behind the graveyard, I paused and attended to the case at my side.

The right moment that Mr. Brody had spoken of had to be now. I grasped the flap — but it still wouldn't budge. I slid the box off my pajama belt so I could wrestle it with both hands.

"Come on," I said. I pried. I put it on the ground and pinned it with one foot, but it held as firm as a honey jar lid.

I didn't know what to do. This would have been a great moment for a pros and cons list.

"Can't open it?" said a voice from nearby. "That's too bad."

A form stepped from behind a nearby tree.

Abe Møller was an old man, of medium build. He was wearing a set of pajamas with vertical blue stripes, and his feet were bare. His face was leathery, with sunken cheeks, and he looked tired, but there was also an unmistakable amusement smoldering in his eyes. More than any of that, though, one other thing distinguished him in the dark, subtle night, which was this: he had snuck up on me. He hadn't been given away by his flux stream, because he didn't have one. There were no flames burning on his head. Where in this strange world you'd normally see the fire, and the flakes pouring out, there was . . . ice. White ice, like a frozen lake—what I'd previously thought was a white hat.

"Think for a moment, young man," said Møller, "about your predicament. I know you're a thoughtful sort. You have two options. One, you give me that box. Two, I take it."

"You can't hurt me," I said. "Subtle forms are invulnerable."

Møller nodded. "That's true," he said. "I can't hurt you here, and I can't hurt your friends. I'm only glad I was able to use them to draw you out, Henry, because it will give what I say next a little more weight."

He paused, and I just stared at him. I knew I couldn't run. I waited, wishing in some part of my mind that, somehow, this could all be stopped. That the clocks would stop ticking. That the world would stop turning.

"Let me tell you a trick I learned, many years ago," Møller continued, as casually as if explaining how to boil an egg. "The trick is separating the subtle form from the physical one, and keeping both of them awake." He waited for this to sink in. Then he said, slowly, his tone going dark, "I am in your house right now, Henry. I am standing by your bed. I may not be able to hurt you here, but I can certainly hurt you there."

I willed myself to wake up at home. I willed that somehow my body there would get up and run off, or that I would cry out for my parents, but I didn't have that kind of skill.

My fear seemed to amuse Møller. "You're weak, my boy, wasting all of your energy on that bonfire." He gestured at the rainbow of my flux stream, twisting above me. "If you could learn to retain that for yourself, as I've done, maybe you'd be strong enough to get out of this fix."

"It's not like that," I said. "You're wrong."

Møller smiled. "Some people say those flakes symbolize friendship. Have you heard that? Yes, some people think your flux spectrum shows your connection to other people—your love for them, maybe. But that's the opposite of what it is. Henry, you have opened your gates to the invaders. The fire you send up is the city of yourself, burning. The influence of others destroys you. Only if you smother it will you survive."

"No, you have to let it burn," I said. "It's . . . it's a distress call." And just then a sound came from behind us.

Møller spun around as a figure stepped from a dense copse of maples.

Funny how earlier when I'd thought that everything was up to me, I'd forgotten about a certain someone.

Mrs. Brody was dressed in a flannel nightgown, and she wasn't stooped as I had always seen her, but was unbent by the years. I noticed something else, too. Her flux stream was like her husband's, deeply diverse, with no clear boundary between one hue and the next, strikingly beautiful.

"My husband sends you his greetings," she said to Møller, "from his graveside, where he's freeing your prisoners."

"That's impossible," said Møller.

"Nothing is impossible," replied Mrs. Brody, "for the one who has the key." She reached into a pocket of her gown and pulled out a small key — pure black, like an obsidian arrowhead.

"Ink!" said Møller. The surprise in his voice was the first real emotion I'd seen in him.

But the surprises were only beginning. To either side of Mrs. Brody, three more people suddenly emerged from the trees — Sergeant Johnson alongside two other uniformed NFTSA agents, a man and a woman.

Møller's eyes widened. He reached with his right hand and pinched himself on the left arm — like you might do in a dream if you wanted to wake yourself.

And he vanished, just like that.

"He's reset himself!" said the sergeant.

"I know where he is," I said, quickly. "He's in my house. But I bet he's running now!"

Sergeant Johnson turned to the other agents. "Reset, and call the local police!"

The other agents did what Møller had done — pinched themselves and disappeared.

And so it was just the three of us, standing in the dark forest.

The sergeant turned to me. "Henry," he said, "you've just handed us the best chance we've had to capture Abe Møller in years. I can hardly believe it. And so I must go, follow my men —"

"No, Sergeant," said Mrs. Brody. "You must stay here. This night is not over yet." She turned to me and smiled. "The alien," she said, "has answered your distress call."

CHAPTER 25

MRS. BRODY LED US quickly into the graveyard. We approached from the rear and arrived steps away from Mr. Brody's fresh grave, where masses of flowers were still piled from his funeral.

"Helen!" I shouted when I saw my sister.

"Henry!" she exclaimed.

Nicki and Alan were there too, and we came together in a big hug, our flux streams boiling up into a squally bonfire. They'd all been trapped, but those jaws were now disarmed and lay sprung and harmless near the grave.

"Henry, I'm so glad you're okay," said Nicki.

"I'm glad you are too," I said. I looked around. "Where's Mr. Brody? Didn't he free you all?"

"He did," said Helen, "but he left. He said he'd come back."

The sergeant approached the four of us. "Excuse me,"

he said, "Henry, are these your friends? Helen Nilsson, Alan Dunn, and Nicki Chen?"

"Everyone, this is Sergeant Johnson," I told them. "He's from NFTSA—who we called."

The sergeant produced three more of the passports and handed them out. "Keep your passport on your person at all times," he recited. "If asked to present it by any representative of NFTSA or other recognized government flux agency, you must comply . . ." he ran through the speech.

"Sergeant," said Alan, "my card looks different from theirs." He held it up, and I read it. It said, "OFFICIAL USFT PASSPORT FOR ALAN M. DUNN, ISSUED IN CONJUNCTION WITH THE SOVEREIGN NEZ PERCE NATION."

"The Nez Perce nation is fully sovereign on the flux plane," said Sergeant Johnson. "It is its own country, with its own laws. But remember that physically, you're still subject to the jurisprudence of the United States, and remain a U.S. citizen."

"That seems kind of confusing," said Nicki.

"It is," the sergeant agreed. Just then, Mrs. Brody approached, and the sergeant turned to her. "I'd like to introduce myself to you officially, ma'am," he said. "I'm

Sergeant Ray Johnson. And I am, well, a big fan of your writing. The International Understanding series had a profound impact on me."

"I'm glad to know it, Sergeant," said Mrs. Brody. "I'm always happy to meet my readers." She paused. "Thank you for coming here when I know duty calls you else-where."

"What's going to happen, ma'am?" asked the sergeant.

"I'm not sure," said Mrs. Brody, "but it's happening now." She gestured at the woods.

We all turned, and I saw the glow farther back in the trees—a colorful, highly variegated flux stream glancing off of branches and leaves. It drew nearer, and then Mr. Brody appeared. I recognized him instantly, still wearing his funeral suit and carrying his violin case. "Greetings, everyone," he said in his thick accent as he stepped from between the nearest trees.

And just behind him was someone else.

"Carl!" Alan cried, as he saw his brother.

Carl was dressed in the same T-shirt and blue jeans I'd last seen him in. Things had changed a little with his flux stream, though. It was still largely white, but there were a few faint strands of colored flakes—green and yellow, like plants coming up through old snow.

Alan rushed forward and Carl caught him and lifted him easily in a bear hug. "Hey, little brother," he said.

Mrs. Brody approached her husband, and they embraced and spoke softly in a language I don't know. The tenderness of it seemed to express something that doesn't exist in English, or that I had never heard, at least.

Awestruck, the sergeant approached Mr. Brody. "Excuse me sir," he said, "I'm Sergeant Ray Johnson. I'd just like to shake your hand, if I may, sir. And I want you to know that whatever I can do for you here, I'm at your disposal."

"It's nice to meet you, Sergeant," said Mr. Brody. "I'd like to introduce you to a friend of mine. This is Carl Dunn." He turned to Carl, who was standing at his elbow.

"Hello," said Carl. He sounded nervous. And he looked, somehow, smaller than normal. Like a scared kid.

"Carl has been the victim of a terrible experiment," said Mr. Brody, "which I'm afraid I'm indirectly responsible for."

"You? I doubt that, sir," said the sergeant.

"Yet it's true," said Mr. Brody. He paused. "Did you catch him, Sergeant? Tell me that, first. Is Abe Møller in custody?"

"I'm afraid I don't know, sir," Sergeant Johnson replied.

"My agents and the local authorities are closing in on the location Henry reported. I have high hopes—higher than I've ever had."

"I'll content myself with your hopes, then," said Mr. Brody. "As to my responsibility for this predicament, Sergeant, allow me to explain. Early in our partnership, when I still mistakenly trusted him, I confided a theory to my friend Abraham—a notion that the subtle form could outlast the physical, given certain preparations. The nature of these preparations I thankfully did not reveal to him."

"And you were correct, sir," said the sergeant. "You've done it! It's a powerful discovery."

Mr. Brody shook his head. "I'd always thought never to test my idea. It seemed an awful kind of knowledge, for it depends on certain very rare subtle ingredients. To what lengths would certain people go to obtain them? Or to prevent others from having them? I did not wish to unleash such a thing upon the world. But when push came to shove, as they say . . ." He turned to his wife. "Maria," he said, "I couldn't bear to leave you."

"I knew you were still there, Joseph," said Mrs. Brody. "But to live like this, invisible, bodiless . . ."

Mr. Brody smiled. "I wish I'd consulted you first," he

said. "It has been no sort of existence, these past days. I've played for you on this violin that you so kindly buried with me. But you cannot hear it." He turned back to the sergeant. "Abraham searches for this secret. He's been stalking it for decades, and my survival now has cemented his curiosity. He came here to observe me, perhaps to study me, and to begin his own experiments. Carl was his unwitting subject. I fear Carl and I are two examples of the same thing."

"Carl . . . ?" said Alan.

Carl tried to smile, but he couldn't. His eyes were full of fear.

"Did Møller say anything, to any of you, about this experiment?" Mr. Brody asked us. "Did he tell you whether Carl was alive or dead? What he had done to him?"

"He told me something," I said. "He said that he . . . that he didn't know. He said we'd interrupted everything."

"Oh, Carl!" said Alan, and he threw himself into his brother's arms. Carl squeezed him back. I could tell he was really scared, what with all of us talking about whether he was dead or not.

Mr. Brody gestured at the sergeant's square satchel. "Do you have with you a field telephone?" he asked.

"Yes, I do."

"Then we're faced with a conundrum," said Mr. Brody. "Whether or not we should request a remote reset for Carl."

"We could do it," said the sergeant, "but . . ."

"If he is still alive somewhere," said Mr. Brody, "perhaps unconscious, or in some kind of prolonged sleep, then he will return to himself and awaken. He will be saved."

"But if his body is dead . . ." noted the sergeant. "If he's like you, Mr. Brody, and we return him to his body . . ."

"He will perish," Mr. Brody finished for him. "That is the choice." He turned to Carl. "To stay here, like this, Carl—a veritable ghost. Or to return. To take the chance on living if you can, knowing that the alternative is death."

Carl looked at Mr. Brody with a quiet intensity, as if the kindly man's gaze was a lifeline. "I . . . I don't know," he said. His voice quaked, and my heart went out to him. It was too awful. I glanced at my friends and saw that they were all speechless. Carl stared into the woods. "I met him in a dream," he said, "or I thought it was." He glanced up at the mostly white streams that were pulsing from him. "He said the colors are like people invading my brain. So you put up walls. Keep them out. It made me stronger at first. But then . . . then I was alone. And now I've even lost myself."

Mr. Brody looked to his wife, who stood next to him, and in his eyes was a question—one he asked her without speaking.

Mrs. Brody nodded. "I know you must, Joseph," she told him.

"Sergeant," said Mr. Brody, "I would like to take a remote reset from you."

"You, sir? But your body is dead. If we reset you to it . . ."

"I understand fully, Sergeant Johnson," said Mr. Brody. "I'm doing it not for myself, but for Carl." He turned toward Carl and Alan, who stood together next to me. "Carl, I'll go ahead of you. And if it's to be your death tonight, I'll be waiting for you when you cross over. You and I will go together, to whatever follows this life."

Carl stared at him. I could tell Mr. Brody's offer stunned him. Really, it was the most generous thing I'd ever heard of—dying just to keep another person company if they had to die too. Finally Carl said, "Thank you, sir." And he stood a little straighter. I could tell he had the courage now to try to find his life again.

"Oh, Joseph," said Mrs. Brody. She put one hand tenderly on her husband's cheek. No sooner had they reunited than they would part once more.

Mr. Brody knelt and opened his violin case. He lifted the instrument, which glowed amber in the moonlight. He began to play. His opening long note harmonized with the branches that scraped in the distance, and it went up from there, ascending into a beautiful melody. It was unlike anything I'd ever heard before. We all listened, and the whole graveyard seemed awake to it. I remembered those forgotten graves Mrs. Brody had told us about—the Jewish graves in Poland, where she was from. The music was so beautiful, I thought Mr. Brody must be playing for those people, too.

The last note died away. Mr. Brody placed the violin on the ground. He nodded to the sergeant, who took his case from his shoulder, unbuttoned the top flap, and reached in to retrieve the phone. He dialed. Soon, a quiet voice spoke over the earpiece. I couldn't hear every word, but I recognized the recording, asking if the caller needed a remote reset. To dial 1.

Mr. Brody turned to his wife, and they held each other. Then he took the receiver from Sergeant Johnson. "I have nothing to fear," he said. "I know my friends will never leave me."

A noise erupted from the earpiece, like hundreds of people applauding.

The receiver fell to the ground.

Mr. Brody was gone, as if he'd never been there at all.

I looked directly behind, at the new grave where the mounded flowers lay. For the first time since that grave had been dug, there was a whole man in it. I felt lucky to have known him.

"Goodbye, my Joseph," Mrs. Brody whispered.

Then Carl knelt and picked up the receiver. "I thought I was going to live forever," he said quietly. "I thought I was . . . that I was the good guy."

I hadn't ever taken much time to consider Carl's perspective on all that had happened, and so it startled me to hear him say this. This bully, who had terrorized every kid in the county and given me an undeserved black eye, thought he was the good guy. But it made sense. Airman Crusader thought he was a good guy. So did Abe Møller.

"Carl, are you sure . . . ?" said Alan. "Maybe you could just stay here, like this."

Carl shook his head. "There's a chance . . ." he began, but he couldn't finish. Suddenly, he started to cry.

He just burst out like he'd been holding it back and then the dam failed. Gulping sobs came out of him, shaking his whole body. He was absolutely terrified. But he was going to go through with it. He held the receiver to his ear.

The sergeant dialed. I heard the woman's voice come on the line, the recording tinny in the earpiece.

"I love you, Carl," said Alan.

"I love you, little brother," Carl replied.

The applause sounded. I was looking right at him when it happened. One moment he was standing there, and the next he wasn't. There was no flash of light, or sound, or anything. The receiver fell to the ground.

The campsite was perfectly still. Off in the forest behind us, the branches creaked. A mixture of moon and star shadows glowed on the ground. I looked at Helen, who's usually the first to snap out of shock over something. She was silent.

In the end, it was not one of us who broke the stillness. It was something else. An unexpected sound—a distant, muffled voice nearby. From Mr. Brody's grave.

We all turned, and I saw something then that I think I will never see again in my life.

Right where the mound of flowers was piled, a sudden disturbance knocked a few of them to lower ground. And there, stark in the moonlight, was a human hand, grasping desperately. I recognized those fingers — had seen them up close as they came at my face only a few days ago. They were Carl's.

Alan cried out and rushed forward, but there was nothing he could do. In his subtle form, he could touch nothing.

The hands clawed at the earth as at the edge of a cliff. The arms lunged out to the elbows, scattering the blooms. Then Carl's head and shoulders emerged, shuddering into the night. Both of him were there, one right inside the other — his subtle form and his physical form together at last.

He cried as he struggled up from the earth, gasping, finally rolling up onto the dirt to lay exhausted, his chest heaving.

We stood around him, powerless. I found myself holding hands with Nicki and Mrs. Brody, and they held hands with Helen and Sergeant Johnson, who both linked arms with Alan so that we formed a ring.

Carl was at the center, in his T-shirt and blue jeans. He had no shoes on, and every inch of him was caked in dirt. He lay there, breathing in gusts and crying. Slowly, though, his breathing became more shallow, and he calmed down.

Then he sat up and listened intently to the night. "Are you here?" he whispered. There was no reply — or none that he could perceive. He choked and coughed, and dirt and spit splashed from his muddy lips. He put his hands on his knees and slowly pushed himself to his feet. He took a hesitant step forward, then another. Our invisible circle parted to let him through.

"I'm going . . ." he said. He took another step. "I'm going . . . to be different." His voice cracked. "No more," he said. "No more . . ." His path brought him to the edge of the graveyard, and he limped on, past the gate toward the road.

We stood together, still holding hands, listening to Carl's retreating footsteps and the slow drone of the forest. From overhead, the stars shone on the empty dirt, strewn with blossoms.

I swallowed hard and turned to Nicki. Her subtle face was lit by the gentlest moonlight.

"Nicki," I said.

She turned to me, her eyes shining. "What is it, Henry?" she asked.

"Would you, that is . . . um, would you want to, um . . . go to the Fall Formal with me?"

She smiled. "I thought you'd never ask," she said.

Then, to my right, Helen said, "Alan, you're taking me, too, okay?"

"Okay," said Alan, wiping tears from his cheeks. He smiled. "I'd like that."

CHAPTER 26

THIS YEAR'S FALL FORMAL THEME was "Making Dreams a Reality," and everyone was supposed to dress up like a character from a fairy tale.

My friends and I planned to do one better.

The afternoon beforehand, Helen and I dressed up — not as fairy tale people, but just as ourselves. I put on a dark blue suit with a red tie. Helen wore a dark blue sleeveless dress. (Yes, we both wore dark blue because we are twins.)

"You two look wonderful," said Mom, and Dad nodded his agreement.

While we were putting on the finishing touches in the downstairs bathroom, a knock sounded at the front door. None of us were expecting a visitor, and Dad went out, thinking it was probably a salesman. But then he didn't come back. Eventually I said, "Is Dad still out front? Who's he talking to?"

Mom went to see. She didn't come back either.

Finally, Helen and I investigated.

The conversation happening in the kitchen was wrapping up as we entered. We were both surprised to see Joe Chen, Nicki's father.

Joe was a short man with thinning hair. He was just stepping out through the screen door as we entered, and my dad was saying, "Thanks again, Joe."

"Yes, thank you so much," said Mom.

"Oh, hello, Henry, Helen," said Mr. Chen, pausing as he held open the screen door. "Well, you're both looking very grown-up."

"Thank you, sir," I said. I hadn't met Nicki's dad many times, and I wanted to make a good impression. I was glad I was wearing a suit.

"Well, see you all soon," said Mr. Chen, and he stepped the rest of the way out the door and walked to his truck.

As soon as he was gone, Mom and Dad turned to each other and shared an astonished look.

"What is it?" I said.

"What happened?" said Helen.

Dad turned to us. "That was your friend Nicki's father," he said.

"We know that," said Helen.

"There's a job opening at Bell Telephone," said Dad.

"And he . . . recommended me for it. I'll interview on Monday."

"Wow, that's great!" I said.

"Yes," said Dad, shaking his head as if he could hardly believe it.

I stood there recalling the night at Mrs. Brody's house when I told Nicki why I'd been forbidden to see her. I figured she must have told her dad. And instead of getting angry . . . he'd decided to help.

Helen and I left home on our bikes around sunset, and we did not pedal toward school, as we'd told Mom and Dad we would. We went in the opposite direction, out the highway to South Half, and followed the bumpy lane to the Brody mansion.

Alan and Nicki were already there. Nicki was wearing a pink dress with spaghetti straps. I can't describe it any more than that, because there was no way I could get up the guts to look closer.

Alan was dressed like me, in a suit. His was slate gray, and he wore a black tie. His shoes, like mine, were shiny. We'd rented them from the same place.

Mrs. Brody was there too, though she wasn't dressed up.

And one other person, who I hadn't expected—Sergeant Johnson.

Needless to say, we were all excited to see him.

"Sergeant, did you catch him?" said Helen, immediately keen to know.

"It's nice to see you too," he replied.

"Let's sit and enjoy some chamomile tea," said Mrs. Brody. Leading the way, she soon seated us around the dining table with steaming cups in our hands—well, not soon. Now that she was in her physical body, Mrs. Brody had returned to her extremely slow way of doing things. We all lent a hand with cups, tray, and teapot.

"My young friends," said the sergeant as he placed his cup of tea on the table, "I want to thank you all for the important role you've played in recent events. Without you, we would never have known that Abe Møller was here. Without you . . . we never would have captured him." He smiled.

"You did it!" said Helen. She banged the table triumphantly with both hands.

"Abe Møller is in custody," the sergeant continued, "and awaiting trial for more than three decades of crimes, including the most recent ones committed in Farro." He paused. "I can't tell you how happy I am. I can think of no way to adequately express my gratitude, but I have brought a small token from my department." He opened a case he had with him, and retrieved a stack of papers. He passed them out, one sheet to each of us. They were official recommendations from NFTSA, endorsed by the director of the department as well as by the sergeant.

It was weird to get something like that—something so tangible, after such an intangible adventure.

"Henry," said Sergeant Johnson, "you've got an odd expression on your face. Is something troubling you?"

"Well, I guess it's just, you know . . . we didn't get to see him captured. It's like a book with a missing chapter."

"Like not getting to see Airman Crusader face down the centipede king?" said the sergeant, with a wink.

"You've read *Airman Crusader*?" I said, surprised.
"Sure," said the sergeant. "Don't get me wrong, they're terrible books in some ways. But they're exciting." He paused. "We aren't cutting off any heads here, Henry. The rule of law demands due process in the courts. And as bad as he is, Abe Møller is still a man. His rights mustn't be stripped from him. Tell me, would you really want it any other way?"

The sergeant spoke the truth. Even though it was strange to hear about Møller's capture after the fact, I was glad he would get a fair trial.

"Henry," said Sergeant Johnson, "what ever happened with the box—the one Joseph Brody gave you? Did it open? Did you find out what was inside?"

"No, I never did," I said. "It's still on my belt, in the subtle world. And I still don't understand why I couldn't open it in the forest. If it was a weapon like Mr. Brody said, why not let me use it against Møller? I'm starting to wonder if there's something wrong with the lock."

"That's possible," said the sergeant, but I could tell he doubted it. It seemed unlikely that Mr. Brody would have made such a mistake.

We spent some time talking with Sergeant Johnson about everything that had happened, and we laughed about some of our close calls. Now that the adventure was over, things that seemed pretty scary at the time were starting to seem almost fun.

Before long, though, it was time to go to bed. Well, time for us, anyway. The sergeant left and Mrs. Brody showed us into the living room, where the couches were all pushed near to one another as they had been for our previous sleepover. This was the plan — to go to the dance as our subtle selves.

"You all look beautiful," said Mrs. Brody. "Let me get my camera."

We stood by the living room windows for the photo. Mrs. Brody snapped the shutter and wished us a good dance. Then we turned out the lights, lay down on our couches, and propped up our arms.

1, 1, 2, 3, 5, 8, 13 . . .

CHAPTER 27

ONCE WE'D ROLLED OUT of our bodies, we walked out of South Half to the highway, but we didn't go straight to school. Alan said, "Let's stop by my house. There's something I want to check on." He wouldn't tell us what.

As we walked, I held Nicki's hand. I still hadn't really looked at her. I glanced her way and shook my head, hardly able to believe that we were on a date. Then I glanced again. Yes, she was still there.

At Alan's house I saw a few people in the field out front. One had a flux stream that was threaded through with white—Carl. But there was more color than ever. He was changing, just like he'd said he would.

Carl was holding a baseball bat. Behind him was someone crouching with a catcher's mask on his head and a mitt on one hand. Out on the pitcher's mound was a third figure.

"Is that Mr. McTavish?" said Helen of the man with the mask. I looked closely. Yes, it was McTavish for sure.

"Where did Carl get a subtle baseball bat?" I asked.

"He went to sleep with it in his hands," said Alan.

I should have thought of that. Whatever you're wearing when you go to sleep is what you wake up with. Even a baseball bat. I squinted out at the third figure, the one on the pitcher's mound. Finally I recognized Mr. Dunn. But he wasn't hunched over from his messed-up back. He was still a big guy, with somewhat of a gut on him, but he stood straight. In one hand he held a baseball, and the other hand wore a glove. I guess he had gone to sleep holding them too.

"You told your dad?" Helen said, surprised.

"Why not?" said Alan. "And he told McTavish."

Helen and I glanced at each other, imagining telling our own parents and totally unsure whether we should. I wondered what it would be like to be subtly grounded.

Mr. Dunn leaned back, brought his arm around, and lobbed a pitch at Carl. It was slow, and for a second it seemed like it would be an easy hit. But as the ball passed over the plate, it dropped out of the air like a stone. Carl swung and missed, and the ball sank right into Mc-Tavish's mitt.

"Wow!" I said. "Was that a knuckleball?"

"He's going to pitch again," said Alan, a little choked up.

I'm happy to report that Nicki looked incredibly beautiful that night in her frilly pink dress as she did a swan dive off the roof of the school. At least, out of the corner of my eye she did.

We all jumped, by the way—even me. And it was pretty fun, as Helen had claimed. I did it twice.

Then we went to the dance.

The gymnasium was full of kids dressed right out of a fantasy world—princes and princesses, ogres, dragons, a toad. A cardboard castle sprawled across the floor, and there was a big bowl of punch labeled "MEAD." But no one there was as convincing as we were. We were ghosts—real ghosts. Invisible.

The music was mostly fast songs, rock and roll tunes that we could jump around to—but I was feeling nervous. Ever since that day when I saw Nicki dancing, I'd worried what would happen if a real dance song came up.

As the evening wore on and some of the kids started to leave, the DJ began playing slower numbers. Then he leaned into his mike and said, "Time for our last song. Let's do a slow dance to Elvis Presley singing 'Are You Lonesome Tonight?'"

The music started. I'd always thought this song was strange and eerie, but now I felt I finally understood it. It's about love — about how missing a person means you love them. It made me think of the Brodys, and how much they'd loved each other. That kind of loneliness, I thought, is a good kind. It means you care about someone.

"Nicki," I said, looking at the floor, "I don't know how to dance."

Without a word, she took my right hand and placed it on the small of her back, and grasped my left hand with her right. "Don't step on my feet," she said, smiling.

Our subtle forms moved close.

"I really like you, Nicki," I said.

"I like you, too, Henry," she replied.

And I finally looked at her. It was maybe the bravest thing I ever did, and also the best. I can't describe it. Maybe if I knew another language, I could find the words.

I leaned forward and kissed her. A subtle kiss is a strange thing. It's slippery, and a little electric, and it buzzes on your lips. And it makes a little "click" sound.

Click?

Nicki felt it too. "What was that?" she said. Then, "Henry — the box!"

I looked down at my side. There was the box, as always . . . but the flap at the top was no longer fixed. It had opened.

A little hesitantly, I reached in. I heard a gasp right next to me, and looked to see Helen and Alan there, with expressions of astonishment.

"What's inside, Henry?" said Alan.

I pulled my hand out.

I was holding a book. It was a hardback, with a blue fabric cover. Even as I looked at it, a few small, colored snowflakes broke away from it and floated off into the room — blue, yellow, red, brown.

Around us, our classmates circled slowly as Elvis sang. They had no idea we were there, and, for the moment, we had no idea about them either. I opened the book, and my eyes ran over the words on the first page — only a few, but they defied understanding. I read them again.

THE TRAP
By Henry Nilsson

The rest of the pages—maybe three hundred of them—were blank.

There was one other thing in the box. I brought it out so my friends could see.

It was a fountain pen with a long slender shaft leading to a gold point. And there, poised at the tip, glistened a drop of black ink.

"Henry," Helen whispered, "you're going to have to, um . . . I mean . . ."

I knew what she was trying to say.

My heart fluttered in my chest, and the pen felt shaky in my fingers. The whole universe unfolding, Mr. Brody had said—like a story written out.

I was going to have to think about this.

ACKNOWLEDGMENTS

Novels aren't easy to produce, even in the best of circumstances. During the course of composing this story, I learned that when the going gets tough it's the people around you who make or break your efforts. I was immensely fortunate in this case to be buoyed by some excellent makers.

I'd like to thank my agent, Jenni Ferrari-Adler, not only for her invariably sage advice and well-grounded strategizing around my literary life, but also just for sticking with me, especially when my circumstances periodically grew incompatible with the writing of books. I'd also like to thank my editor Margaret Raymo at HMH, not only for devoting so much time to the many rounds of revision this story required and for constantly pressuring me with better ideas and insightful questions, but also for her patience with my "two steps forward, one step back" creative process.

As its opening sentence attests, this book is set in 1963. It's a year that occurred a decade before I did. While I tried to get a sense of things by reading blotty scans of old newspapers, I also wrote a letter that began, "Dear Person Who Was Alive In 1963 . . . " I'd like to thank everyone who responded, whether briefly or at length, to the questions I asked, especially Oliver, Maria, Peter, and Jack—I think I said to one of you, "You have just written my book for me." I didn't really mean that, though, and I'm going to keep whatever money I make from it. I am nonetheless deeply indebted to you for opening such brilliant windows on things I never saw.

Above all others, no matter how deserving they may be, I'd like to thank my wife, Anne. When we married sixteen years ago, there was a lot of talk about "better or worser, richer or poorer," but I find that terminology mistaken. You've given me better in the midst of worser, and poor times I count as rich because of our life together. Thank you for this strange, impossible daily alchemy.

Last, to my readers, thank you for reading. I've spent a large part of my life struggling to be a better writer, and it hasn't gotten easier. It's profoundly encouraging to see my efforts turned into real stories in the imaginations of people who are committed to seeing the best in them.